WOMAN KING

BOOK 3 OF THE TERRAFOLK TRILOGY

FRANCESCA CRISPO

IBSN: 979-8-9885719-4-0

Cover illustration by Melissa Hudson - www.mhudson-illustration.com

Editing and proofreading by Three Fates Editing - www.threefatesediting.com

Formatting by Nezhda Seyfulova - www.nezhformatting.org

CONTENTS

CONTENT WARNING

Birth/labor, breastfeeding, kidnapping of a child, murder, death, active war/battles, use of weapons, gore, suicidal ideation and suicide, reference to previous sexual assault, reference to loss of a partner, graphic descriptions of sexual activity, postpartum depression/anxiety.

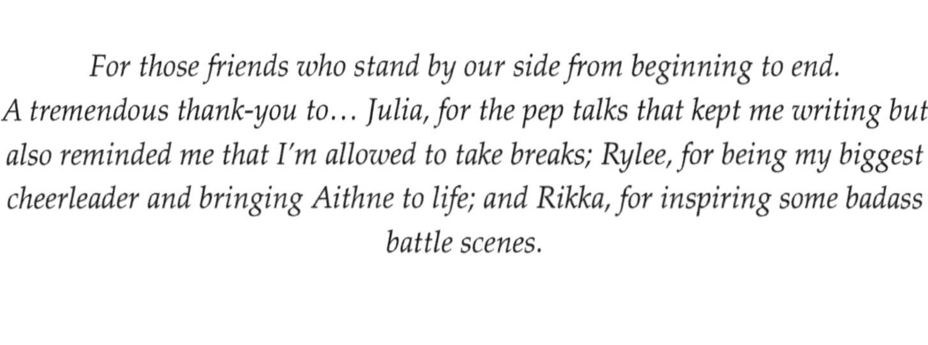

*For those friends who stand by our side from beginning to end.
A tremendous thank-you to… Julia, for the pep talks that kept me writing but also reminded me that I'm allowed to take breaks; Rylee, for being my biggest cheerleader and bringing Aithne to life; and Rikka, for inspiring some badass battle scenes.*

WINTER

"*E*vren Firth, prince of the land and sea."

Mycel was so stoic when she announced the baby's name, having roared him into the world only moments before. She no longer seemed like the quirky roommate I'd gotten to know in Seattle, but the just and powerful ruler of an entire civilization. A ruler, and now a goddess, a bringer of life. The moment the crown had snapped from its creating branches and settled onto her head, she had changed. It was almost as though the air around her had shifted. Gone was her naive curiosity about humans and their strange ways; gone was her carefree attitude. And yet, she'd still danced with me; she'd still pressed her forehead to mine and reminded me that I was her best friend, her platonic soulmate, and that she loved me, that she saw me and felt both my pain and joy. That was Mycel: complex, multifaceted, and undoubtedly the only person who could win this fight to save her people and humankind. Though my heart ached for the simplicity of what once was – when our biggest worry had been making rent, a foreign concept now – I felt honored to be by her side in this journey.

Her regulating breaths filled the treehouse with condensation in the freezing winter air, and calm settled amongst us all once we were certain that both baby and mama were healthy and safe. I'd never witnessed the birth of new life and wasn't sure if terrafolk magick affected the ease of the process, but Mycel made it seem intuitive. The way the body tears itself apart to make way for another being is raw and violent, but Mycel still behaved as if she was programmed to do it. How did she do that? How did she harness the strength to carry on, even when the world seemed to be on the verge of ending? And now, here she was so selflessly giving her child the name of my lost lover and our dear friend.

All I could muster was a teary nod of appreciation in response to her announcement. Firth's loss was too fresh still, a gaping hole in my chest that could be seen by anyone who approached me. I was raw and bleeding. It felt like it might be that way forever. Could they hear the wind blowing through that wound? Could they see the fragile, unsure beating of my heart within its tattered case? If I were jostled too hard, it might just be the end for me; I was barely holding it together. It was no wonder that very few terrafolk had approached me since our arrival at Yannava, even when I felt like I was putting on a brave face.

I stood in silence as the little one curled up against his mother's chest, finally sleeping after the chaos of being ushered earthside, and I peeked into his bundled blanket to stroke his cheek. So warm and tender was Evren Firth. There was a tuft of light hair already atop his round head. He looked nothing like my mountain of a man – he was light and soft, whereas Firth had been dark and brutish, at least on the outside – but the shared spirit was there. In his few waking moments he had made intense eye contact with his mama: focused, intentional, and curious. He even gave me a small glance through his new eyes, but I still couldn't speak to him in response. His alertness and the intensity of his gaze surprised me; weren't babies supposed to be bleary-eyed little creatures with no awareness of their surroundings?

Maybe it was his magickal blood. I hoped that, one day, there would be a tenderness in my heart for him that was based on love and not just longing for what could have been. This new life deserved to exist free of the looming shadows of its predecessors.

When Mycel's gaze finally met mine, she offered me a solemn half smile. "You don't have to stay."

I pressed my forehead to hers once more, needing to show her that I was still there, even if it seemed, at times, that I was a million miles away. I closed my eyes and took a steadying breath before facing her gaze again. I wanted to stay, but I couldn't. "You did it, Sprout. I love you." I cast Earwyn one last glance. "I wish you could have a celebratory drink with him. He would be so proud, ya know?"

Clove, who had been a silent and understanding observer once Evren was earthside, gave me a knowing nod as I headed for the door of the treehouse. Her presence reminded me of my own mother, who I hadn't seen in years; I missed her, and I had no clue when I would be able to get in touch with her again, let alone how she'd react when her packages started being returned with a note about the wrong address. I prayed that she didn't think I was dead, or worse, that I was trying to abandon her. It was outlandish, though, the situation I was in, and I couldn't just give her a call to explain that I was now part of a war and that I didn't know when I'd see her again, if ever. With a battle on the horizon, I felt no urgency to contact her. Who knew what ties the Ulmosi had? They'd killed Firth… if they knew about my mother, would they go searching for her, too? The Ulmosi's disregard for human life cemented my decision to keep my distance from any living relatives or friends I had in the human world; it wasn't worth the risk. I could mend relationships when the time came.

Soon, Earwyn would step out of the treehouse to announce the baby's birth. I would not, could not, be there when the crowd of Yannavi rallied and cheered, if that was the sort of thing they did. The cries of "Evren Firth, our prince" would shatter me; Firth, the first

Firth, deserved that sort of celebration for his sacrifices. After that, who knew what would happen? I'd never been part of a war before, I didn't know how this would play out or how it would end. The thought of dying in battle didn't faze me, and suddenly I understood what Mycel must have felt when she attempted to float off with the sea months before. All I knew was that the memory of Firth was everywhere, for better or worse – a reminder that we hadn't had enough time. But what time is enough with the person you love the most? It would only have been enough if we departed this mortal plane together after decades of adventure and passion and laughter; nothing less would have sufficed.

I had been plunged into an unbelievable world with little to hang on to besides my best friend and a soft, sweet man the size of a mountain. Now that the time to fight had come, I only had one left; I'd protect that one with my life, because going on alone just wouldn't be an option. I was angry. Hurt. Reckless.

I opened the door of the treehouse only to run straight into Reed, Mycel's ex-lover. I hit his body hard, and he caught me by the arm before I stumbled over the railing of the elevated abode. "Alright there?" he asked, setting me upright like I weighed nothing. Oh, god, maybe I wouldn't stand a chance in a fight against people like him; if they could pick me up and toss me around with ease, it was hard to see what I might bring to the fight. Grit, maybe, but that wasn't enough to keep myself or others alive. And what was it with these giant men being everywhere? Why was this one touching me? I wished he wouldn't; it felt wrong that any man other than Firth should touch me again. I couldn't think of it. Goosebumps exploded across my skin, and my stomach rolled, every fiber of my physical being rebelling against the unwelcome contact.

"I'm fine," I told him, without bothering to meet his stare. It was hard for me to look people in the eye lately. I shrugged out of his grasp without thinking and gestured to the door. "I think they're ready to see you." Before he could respond, I was hurrying down the wooden steps to the forest floor.

Reed tried to call after me. "Are you sure you're—"

I didn't look back. Instead, I shoved my hands into my pockets and walked into the center of Yannava. I still hadn't gotten accustomed to the biting cold of the forest; there was something different about being out in the wilderness and exposed to the elements versus navigating Seattle streets in the winter, where every new corner held the promise of warm coffee shops and bookstores. I was bundled in layers of clothing from the Yannavi, but even so, the chill reached my bones. Mycel's people were clearly used to the changing temperature of the forest and didn't need thick layers of fabric to insulate them, but the fact that they noticed my need touched me. The people of Yannava seemed to yearn for connection with everyone, animals, humans, and other terrafolk alike. Now that they weren't under the rule of Mycel's tyrannical aunt, I could see the true extent of their warmth and hospitality.

The people of Yannava were bustling, busy with preparations for what was to come, the details of which no one seemed to know. They were probably all holding their breath to learn about the new heir to the throne, too. Firth and I had never discussed kids; we had been so fully enraptured with each other that even though we loved every child we interacted with, I couldn't imagine us having space in our relationship for anyone else. And when I say "loved," I mean "loved"; to see Firth interact with a child was like seeing a sky full of rainbows. For such a big lug, he was gentle and sweet and soft and… just the thought of him holding a little kid's hand in his giant paws caused me to choke back a sob. Maybe we wouldn't have wanted kids, but I mourned the loss of that option.

As I walked through the main gathering area of the wooded city, the space where my best friend had reclaimed the rule of her people only days prior, magick was being used by almost every person I passed. I still wasn't used to how commonplace it was here. I'd been plunged into this world with no warning and in such perilous circumstances that I hadn't been able to appreciate it as much as it deserved. But as I walked, I saw the many wonders of the Yannavi.

Young children, younger than Neeri even, manipulated dirt and rocks and branches without touching them, creating intricate structures in the cold winter air. Some used their powers to tend to the animals that lived within the city, providing them with food and water. One rambunctious little girl was using her magick to throw a stick that a small squirrel dutifully returned over and over in a game of fetch. Those who were a bit older used their skills to create weaponry. The sight felt oddly out of place here. Had they ever wielded a sword or dagger like the ones they were creating, or were they just following a blueprint provided by an elder? I prayed that these children would never be on the receiving end of weapons such as these.

The click of stones and bark was loud and crisp against the heavy silence in the air, but was also accompanied by the squish of mud under their feet and shoes. More and more of the ground was getting soft and mushy from the creeping floodwaters. The adults, keeping a watchful eye on the children from afar, worked together to discuss their plans to protect Yannava. One of them created a makeshift map of the land in a patch of dry dirt with a few simple flicks of their wrists. They stood around the map and made suggestions for areas of reinforcement, each of them adding to the map, while the others approved or denied the suggestions. I wondered if they normally watched their children so closely or if it was just due to the impending war. Did the kids know what war was? Were they frightened?

"…are the treehouses big enough to hold all of the children if the forest floods that high?"

"…not sure… Mycel mentioned more Alaskans…"

"Will they have time to teach everyone to swim? Even so, how long can we stay afloat for?"

"If we can't swim or last in the treehouses for long, then we'll be forced to surrender."

"Hyssop said…"

I cringed as I remembered the time Firth had nearly killed my best friend in order to allow her to breathe underwater. Once we'd pulled her sopping-wet body from the tub and I'd held her hair as she vomited salt water and blood into our toilet, we helped her to her bed to recover. We didn't know then that she'd been pregnant; hell, we hadn't known whether she would survive our attempt to give her gills. Looking back, I realized just how reckless it had been, but Mycel would not have taken no for an answer. If she had, we would not have recovered Earwyn, nor would we be at war with his people. Whether Firth would still be alive, however, was hard to say. Once we made sure she was going to live, Firth and I had to talk.

"Were you ever going to tell me?" I had signed to Firth, who was still healing from his wounds but couldn't escape my frustration with his tactful omission of truth. I'd taken to only signing with him, rather than signing and speaking like I did when we were around Mycel and Earwyn. Ulmosi Sign Language had its intricacies and quirks, but I picked it up pretty quickly, and then we had what felt like our own secret language. Other humans didn't know it, at least, and Earwyn had the good sense to look the other way when we conspiratorially or flirtatiously signed to each other in his presence. Like ASL, USL didn't translate directly into English, but for the sake of sharing our conversations, I'll report it as such. "Ya know, about the fact that you're from a magickal kingdom in the ocean and you have superpowers? And the whole rogue prince, feuding kingdoms thing? Any of that?" I struggled a little to recall the Ulmosi signs for magick, prince, and kingdom; they varied from ASL, and admittedly, we had not used them much in our day-to-day conversation. He seemed able to piece my message together, though.

Firth let out a sigh. "Of course I was, Zara," he replied, tracing a "z" over his nose. I'd never seen him sign that before, nor did it align with any signs I knew. It took me a moment to reply until I realized that he'd mixed the sign for "funny" with his traced letter "z."

"Wait, did you just give me my own sign name?" My eyes widened in surprise.

Firth smirked. He knew what he was doing, but I didn't care; it didn't take much for him to melt my frosty moods, despite how hard I tried to fight his charms. "Do you like it?"

"I love it," I signed. I squealed, and it took all of my effort not to jump up and down. The harsh reality of our predicament faded away, at least for the time being. "And you like me enough to give me a sign name."

My hunk of a man laughed.

I raised an eyebrow. "What's so funny? Don't think this means we aren't going to talk."

"Of course I like you enough to give you a sign name, Z. I love you." The look on his face was so matter of fact, so "duh," so "we've already been over this," but we hadn't. That was the first time he told me he loved me. Whereas Mycel and Earwyn had been so transparent with their feelings from day one, we hadn't really put words to ours; the constant time spent together and comfortability around each other had, thus far, been enough to show each other how much we cared. But now that I'd almost lost him… oh god, I'd almost lost him. I struggled to find the words to reply. When I didn't sign a response right away, he added, "You don't have to say it back. I know you love me, too."

He was right.

CHAPTER TWO

MYCEL

$\mathcal{M}$agick or not, children leave their mark. It's reassuring, in a way, that they permanently ingrain themselves into the history of your body and your soul, whether through stretch marks and scars or the memory of their gaze first meeting yours. That gaze… when both of you are exhausted and drained, but running on the fuel of pure love and excitement… is something else.

I had never thought much about having children, never imagined dedicating myself to someone else in the way that I was to Earwyn, Yannava, and now Evren Firth. It was shocking the amount of love I had for that small being upon first sight. He was beautiful, just like his father, and everything it took me to bring him earthside, the pain but also the love from Earwyn and Zara and Clove throughout, made it that much sweeter when his tiny hand gripped my finger at last.

Earwyn had stood by dutifully, silent and supportive, quickly getting whatever I needed at any given moment. He brought water, helped me switch positions when I needed to, and didn't flinch when I gripped his shoulders with all my might or felt it necessary to work through the pain by screaming. He was reserved, neutral, aside from the way his brows knitted together in the moments where I felt like I just couldn't do it, like my body wasn't ready to bring our baby earthside.

"I can't," I'd told him, trying to catch my breath between contractions. Never in a million years could I have imagined that childbirth would be such a test of my fortitude. It's strange to think of it that way, as if I had a choice in the matter. Your body screams at you and tells you it's too much, but you must press on, or it will do so for you. "I can't do this."

He kissed the back of my hand, stroking it with his thumb, his stormy eyes trained on mine. "You can. You were made for this, just like you were made to rule Yannava and to lead your people to victory."

Zara and Clove, meanwhile, puttered around to step in and support whenever possible. The memory of Zara pressing her forehead to mine in silent encouragement as I pushed would be permanently ingrained in my soul; I hoped to one day return the favor to her, if she so desired. Clove was a doting parent figure, wiping my forehead with a damp cloth, stroking my hair, and in the end, catching Evren Firth and bringing him up to my chest so I could hold him when the time came.

I was certain nothing could have been more breathtaking than our first moment of connection – until I let Earwyn hold him and saw the absolute wonder in his gaze, not to mention the relief. Seeing me in pain, wondering if our child and I would both be safe, be healthy, I'm sure it had taken a toll on Earwyn. I imagined he also feared our child would be anything but as perfect as he was, what with the self-doubt that constantly plagued him. But now, as he held our child, safely earthside, as he stared into Evren Firth's bright and sparkling eyes... I could see the tension leave his body.

Zara's reaction to Evren Firth's arrival, and our choice to honor Firth with his name, meanwhile, had caused my heart to ache. I would need to find a slice of time for us to reconnect. I imagined the tender soreness of being reminded of the man she had lost; even I, with my limited time with Firth, had longed for the brief moments of reunion that the rest of our troop got with him. When I'd last seen him alive and well, I was promising that I'd be back soon and that everything would be okay. I had left them with the optimistic hope that life would go back to normal once I returned, that they would be able to live out their days together in goofy bliss, that things could go back to how they had been prior to Earwyn and me losing our magick. I never had a chance to apologize for my failure or to show Firth all the ways I was planning to make it right. Wherever he was, I hoped that he could see Evren Firth as himself living on through another; sure, they'd be very different, but a name was a powerful thing. As Earwyn returned Evren Firth to my arms, somehow, I knew this little being would live up to the name he shared with our lost friend.

There was no time for dwelling on those who were gone, however, when the people in front of me needed tender care. "Tell me how you're feeling," I said to Earwyn, my voice cracked and parched from panting and exhaustion. My eyes burned with the sweat that had dripped into them for hours prior. My body was fatigued, aching for rest, but my mind was buzzing. "Please." Earwyn didn't look at me directly, but immediately reached for the bedside table to fetch a glass of water for me. He offered it to me before responding with a weak laugh. "Don't you think we should be focused on how you're feeling? After all, you did just do all of that work." His voice was low, almost secretive. He glanced at me briefly before looking back at our son, who was now nestled against my bare chest, our bodies warming each other despite the frigid winter air surrounding us. The treehouse we were staying in, which had quickly been claimed as "ours," was small, but beautiful, just like every home in Yannava. Like the dwellings on the ground, it was built in a way that suggested the trees had simply conspired to grow together into a house, like nature knew what we needed and just made it happen for us. There were ample "windows," or rather the frames of windows, which let in light and the occasional critter or tree branch. They were covered with heavy curtains that had been woven by the Yannavi people from varied fibers: either reeds, hemp, or animal fiber from those that the Yannavi people cared for, that were dyed with berries, flowers, or other natural items grown in the forest.

The dwelling seemed to have filled with gifts from my people overnight: jugs of lilac wine and dandelion beer; jars of soups, dried fruits, and jams; breads and mushrooms. In addition to all of the food, well-loved hand-me-downs from the villagers' own children had been washed and carefully wrapped for us as well. There were tunics and pants, all made with the same loving care as the bedding and curtains in the dwelling, as well as bibs, hats, socks, and more. We had no clue what was coming for us and what the coming days would look like, but I hoped that each of us would be left with our homes intact and our beds still a safe place to rest our weary heads. It was a relief to have a landing pad after such a long time without one. Part of me longed for our old apartment, while another missed the amenities of the villas on Aolan, but nothing felt quite as "right" as being home again, even with the war on the horizon. Now I just needed to protect that home.

I sipped the water as I watched Earwyn, appreciating the sensation of the cold liquid over my parched tongue. Labor had been exhausting, body-breaking work, and I thought to myself that I'd never take a full breath or glass of water for granted again. I thought over my words for a moment. "What I mean is, we never really had a chance to talk about it, Wyn… but I know it must be hard seeing your child."

He swallowed hard and side-eyed me in mock incredulousness, as if to say *What kind of monster do you think I am?* But we both knew that I saw nothing monstrous about my husband, in fact, quite the opposite. "Why would you say that?"

"I can only imagine that you've had nightmares about this moment, but with Maren in my place instead. Maybe you... worried that you would resent the child because of what created it or that you'd hate yourself for loving it anyway." I wanted to be gentle with him, to be mindful of when and how I asked these heavy questions, but there just wasn't going to be time for us to slowly broach the topic any time soon. I hoped that he would understand. Life, war, it would all continue to move quickly until it concluded in some way; that conclusion could even mean great loss, and I didn't want us to push forward into a fight without addressing the seemingly small details. They mattered. If we had been fighting anyone but the kingdom of the woman who assaulted him, I might have had a different approach with my husband. When he didn't reply, I continued. "Maybe you've been afraid of seeing a baby that looks like her. But look at him; he's the perfect mix of us, just as I saw him on the *Spark*."

Maz chittered next to me and tilted his head as he looked at the baby in my arms. *A little more pink than you two, but yeah, I can see it!* I stifled a smirk in response to his commentary. He was right; little Evren Firth was quite pink, but then again, being brought into the world is the type of ordeal that might leave you flushed. There's probably a reason people don't remember their own birth...

"Motherhood seems to have amplified your boldness, goddess." Earwyn sighed, almost as if my constant prodding was finally starting to wear him down. I had to push forward, though; he didn't even have Firth to talk to about these things anymore. I hoped that one day he would settle in and have those deep, loving friendships once more. I knew that was a lot to hope for. Friendships were hard to come by, even for someone as loving and charismatic as Earwyn, and I didn't know what I'd do if I lost Zara.

"I want to be as gentle as you need, but I also don't want these things to be pushed aside just because we're in the midst of a war." I took another sip, then set the glass down. Earwyn's gaze remained focused on our son. "Look at me, Wyn," I told him. Otherwise, I feared he'd get lost in his own thoughts.

He did. In his eyes I saw the turbulence of the deepest parts of the ocean and something else… a hurricane, tumultuous and intense, with periods of pregnant stillness that left me with bated breath, waiting for the next blow. If he was like this under the influence of mortality, what would Earwyn be like when his magick returned? I had never seen him unleash his full potential, especially not with so much feeling behind it all. Would he fell trees with it? Capsize ships, take down entire armies?

"This child was created by nothing but pure love and devotion. Safety. Warmth. That's all he'll know. That's all I want you to know for the rest of our days," I told him, then hesitated a little before adding, "and you will, as soon as all is said and done." I reached up to trace a finger along his jawline. The depths of his blue eyes shone with fear and hesitation, but also hope. "I love you," I said. "He loves you." Earwyn nodded in a way that suggested he was barely hanging on to his composure. I knew it wasn't the right time, but I couldn't help but push again. "Do you think you're ready to talk about it… about Maren?" I asked finally.

"Bold," Earwyn commented again, squeezing his eyes shut. He exhaled deeply through his nose. "Too bold. Is this really what you want to talk about on our son's birthday? You should be resting, enjoying him."

"You don't have to… and maybe this isn't the right time, but I can feel her eating away at you. Anyone can say she doesn't have the right to do that, that you shouldn't give her the satisfaction, but it's a lot more complicated than just letting her go." Even in all of the time we'd been together, I only knew bits and pieces of their story. I didn't want to imagine all of the complex horrors that made up their time together, but I was watching Earwyn sink under the weight of those pieces, those painful secrets. He was torturing himself, and he'd continue to unless something changed.

"She left her mark. You're right. It's not something you can just let go of. I hate that it's ruining a moment like this," Earwyn said with another sigh, then opened his eyes to look at me. "I'm supposed to be present for you, for our son." I could tell the words felt foreign on his tongue.

I swallowed hard, and a rush of sadness washed over me in a way I hadn't expected. For him to admit just how deeply she'd hurt him… it had always been a painful thought, but now… I tried to blink away the tears that threatened to slip from the rims of my eyes and focused myself on him again. If I let myself imagine Maren and what she might've done to my husband, it would fill me with rage and leave me unable to connect with him the way we were… and I needed to keep that conversation going. It might be one of the last few moments we had alone for a while.

Clove, whom I'd forgotten was even in the room due to my intense focus on my husband and child, slipped out slowly but not before moving a chair to the bedside for Earwyn to sit in. I thanked her silently. He sat and held my hand, but was unable to meet my gaze for long. Instead, he pressed his forehead to the back of my hand when he spoke. "It's disgusting," he said, voice low. "And if you knew the extent of it, you'd be disgusted with me. I think that's why I'm afraid to tell you more… What sort of father can I be, what sort of role model, when that's my past?"

My heart sank. We'd touched on this before. We'd worked to help him reclaim his identity, to reclaim his masculinity and power in the world and in our relationship. I should've known that the process would be lifelong; I didn't mind putting in the work with him, but I wished his relief could come sooner. I shook my head frantically, stopping only when I realized that the movement might wake Evren; that was a new sensation, a new responsibility for me to be aware of now. "I would never," I half whispered, half yelled. We sat in silence for a moment, my heart aching because I had no clue what to say or do. "Do you want to tell me more?" I squeezed his hand a little and stroked his cheek as well as I could with my captured fingers. I stopped myself before offering to simply drop the topic; we'd done that so many times, and she'd cut him so deep, there needed to be another step taken toward his healing.

"It was always bad, forceful," he said finally, his forehead still pressed hard against my hand. "Violent."

I nodded, trying to be brave for him like he had been for me only moments before.

"And I just…"

"What is it?"

He shook his head. "I could never stop myself from…"

I forced myself to speak, partly because I didn't want him to have to recount things so explicitly but partly because I didn't want to hear it; the imagery was too much. My insides churned at the thought of Earwyn's body betraying him and causing him to think he'd enjoyed his repeated assault, allowing Maren to fool him into thinking that what she was doing to him was just or appropriate. "It's not your fault." Ugh, really? That was all I could muster? He was pouring his heart out, and I could barely force out platitudes.

"She made it seem like I wanted it, just because… I can't say." He'd been no stranger to speaking about sex with me, to naming things in a way that might've seemed brash or vulgar to some, so for him to shy away from any of that language highlighted the stark contrast between both relationships.

"You can't control what your body does, Earwyn," I told him, hoping that the eager honesty in my tone delivered my message. I wanted to grab him and hold him close, to shake his fears out of him, but I couldn't. "That doesn't mean you wanted it. That doesn't mean you deserved it."

He was silent for a while before he met my gaze, his eyes red and damp, much like they probably looked during the interactions we were referring to. "Last time, when I was pulled away from our wedding… She made them cut my hair and dressed me up, put her favorite cologne on me. Like a puppet."

Maren of Ulmos had stripped my husband of his wedding attire to dress him up again and assault him; she had violated him and attempted to undermine and violate our union. How many times had that happened while we were separated? It had taken us such a long time to rouse Firth, to get my gills, and to build my confidence enough for me to reach Ulmos. Perhaps if I had gotten to him sooner, I could've prevented some of his abuse, lessened some of his pain.

I was torn on how to respond. Part of me wanted to hold him close and stroke his hair, to reassure him, and the other wanted to fantasize about which one of us would finally kill her when it came to the last battle between Ulmos and Yannava. But Earwyn didn't strike me as wanting revenge, at least not during that conversation. "She'll never do that again, Wonder," I told him with confidence. I forced my trembling lower lip to still; this wasn't about me.

"It was different last time because I'd been with you, because I knew it could be good and safe," Earwyn confessed. "So when I found myself back in Ulmos, back in her bedroom, it felt like a nightmare. It wasn't the norm anymore."

"I know I can't erase what she's done, no matter how much I wish I could protect your heart like that, but—"

"You do protect my heart, Mycel," he said suddenly, his gaze intense once more. "You can't erase it, but every moment with you dulls those memories a little. Still, I worry that they'll always be a part of me."

"I can't imagine that pain, Wonder…"

"I need you to know, though," Earwyn continued. "I can't go back. If I'm captured again, in this war or another, to use as a pawn, I won't go." He looked at me in silence for a moment, as if trying to ensure that I understood the weight of his words. He wiped his face with his hand, hastily ridding his cheeks of the tears that had tumbled down them. "I can't."

It felt selfish, but I wouldn't allow the words to sink in. "That won't happen."

"I need to know you understand what I'm saying, Mycel. My mind, my body, I wouldn't be able to take it again. I'd come back too broken to offer you and Evren anything."

The weight of his statements hit me like an avalanche, and I found my mouth dry again, lips parted but unable to speak. My heart raced and tumbled in panic, in rage, in fear. I would have promised to get him back from any hell, until the end of our days, but he was clearly telling me his limits; if it came down to dying or going back to Ulmos, he would rather die. Unaware of just how acute his pain was, of just how torturous his life there had been, I had to be okay with his limits. I felt sick. "It won't happen, Earwyn." I gritted my teeth at the sugges-tion that he would leave us permanently. I stroked his cheek and tangled my fingers in his wavy hair, which was slowly but surely returning to the length it had been when we first met. I was about to say more, to praise his strength and bravery and pivot from the talk of my soulmate taking his own life, when a knock sounded at the door.

"It's Reed," his voice called.

Earwyn rose to his feet at a speed that surprised me, wiped his face with his hands once more, and went to the door without a comment. There was an exchange, the content of which I couldn't make out because Earwyn had promptly hushed him upon opening the door, and then Reed entered. I watched the two men intently and noted the sudden change in Reed's expression when his gaze went from me to the baby in my arms.

"Hey, Reed." I greeted him, voice soft and quiet. My exhaustion was finally catching up to me, and something about the safety of being with two men that I knew and loved caused my body to calm a little. Part of me felt greedy, that I should be so lucky to have so many people in my life who made me feel safe and protected, while the rest of me just felt grateful. There was an entire village of people who would fight by my side or keep my son safe while I fought, and that was invaluable. I felt warm and safe for the time being, which hadn't happened in a long while. My body recognized it, too, because it sank deeper into the mattress of our bed, and my eyelids became heavy. I yawned.

"Hey." His voice was gruff, harsh, like he'd forced it from his lips with a fight. "So… this is him, huh?" He shifted his stance before crossing his arms across his chest. I'd never seen him look so uncomfortable and out of place, especially not in his own homeland and especially not around me, of all people. This had not been the reception I was expecting.

Earwyn glanced at him in confusion, no doubt wondering where the cocky Reed from a few days prior had escaped to.

"Yeah." I nodded. "Come see him. You could hold—"

"No, um, nah, that's alright. He's sleeping… and you should rest. I just came to… to tell you that somethin's happening, Mycel."

I couldn't place his discomfort. "What is it?"

"The forest… it's, uh, it's flooding faster than we originally thought. Not a lot yet, but the streams are rising a little, and it's creepin' into the woods. I can tell it's them; it's not natural."

I swallowed hard. "How many Yannavi have noticed?" Earwyn glanced between us.

"The ground has been getting soft, but up until now I don't think it's been worrisome. Only a few who know what to look for have noticed. They aren't sounding the alarm yet, though. They're waiting for your plan. But I thought I'd let you know, we're gonna need that plan soon."

I looked from Reed to Earwyn and back again. "Thanks, Reed. Are you sure you don't—" He was out the door before I could finish my question. I couldn't help but stare at the entryway long after he left. Was this another person who needed connection and follow-up from me? Did I have the space in my mind and heart to make that happen while in the midst of a war? I sighed and rested my head against my pillow, Evren thankfully still asleep against my chest, and steadied myself with some deep breaths. I could feel Earwyn's gaze on me as I lay there, but I knew he wouldn't acknowledge Reed's awkwardness, whether he was intentionally avoiding it or just distracted by everything else going on.

When he piped up again, he was back in his seat beside me. "I know you don't want to talk about this, but how are we going to keep him safe if it comes to a fight? It looks like it's headed that way if the water's already starting to rise. He's going to be a target because of who his parents are, and… a baby is a very easy target, Mycel."

Maz chittered, then hopped closer to the baby as if to guard him. *Like hell he will be!*

"He's right, Maz," I told him, glancing from Evren to my familiar and then to my husband, who had been bold enough to bring up a topic I had been avoiding. That wasn't to say that I hadn't had nightmares about it repeatedly as my pregnancy went on. "He'll have to stay with someone."

"Zara?" Earwyn asked.

"She'll want to fight if that's what it comes down to… they all will. And she won't want to be holed up with her thoughts, waiting to see how many more loved ones she loses. But we'll have to keep those who can't fight tucked as safely away as possible," I said, setting my jaw with a nod. That's what was right and fair. Earwyn and I would be at the front lines ourselves, as a sign of devotion and commitment to Yannava, a contrast to the time that I had fled and left them without my guidance.

Earwyn's eyes widened. "And you want to leave Evren with them?"

"We can't believe that he's any more important than the rest of our people, Wyn," I told him, fully committed to each word I said. Sure, to me, my group was the most important, but as a leader I needed to remember the inherent value of every member of Yannava and every living creature. That was part of my connection to the earth. "Each life here has immeasurable value and should be protected as fiercely as we protect our own child." I yawned, exhaustion finally overpowering me, but stayed strong in my convictions. But even as I looked down at Evren Firth, I thought that I had never seen something quite so beautiful. I had to keep him safe. That was easy as long as I had him in my arms, but I wasn't sure if I'd be able to hand him off to someone else, even if it was the right thing to do.

"It's not like that in Ulmos." His tone was clipped, bitter.

I searched his gaze, then tangled my fingers in his again with a squeeze. "They should have kept you safe, Wyn, like we'll keep our people safe."

"Our people…" Earwyn mused.

"Of course," I told him. "This is your home now. These are your people."

CHAPTER THREE

EARWYN

When I brought my son out to meet the people of Yannava, our queen by my side, the welcome we received was overwhelming. There were more people gathered around our dwelling than I had expected, but the arrival of a baby was exciting in and of itself, not to mention the new heir to the throne. Mycel had already told me that her people celebrated babies and children almost excessively, so I shouldn't have been surprised. The Ulmosi had no such traditions. I held the little boy in my arms, bundled in the clothing and blankets that our people had blessed us with, and propped him up so that he was facing the group of people who had gathered in front of our treehouse. Mycel stood next to me, her arm looped in one of mine in solidarity, but also to steady her body, which was still exhausted. "Go ahead," she whispered to me, gesturing to the crowd a little.

I cleared my throat, willing myself to sound like a leader, a role which was new to me despite my previous titles. "People of Yannava, we'd like to introduce you to your new prince, Evren Firth."

When the group erupted in cheers, clapping, and joyous laughter,

Evren blinked slowly and yawned. "You've got to help take care of them," I told my son, stroking his tiny, soft cheek. "They're relying on you." No pressure, little guy.

* * *

OUR SON WAS ONLY THREE DAYS OLD WHEN MYCEL INSISTED SHE ATTEMPT to return my magick.

"I'd been meaning to try the second I took the throne," she told me. I believed her; I knew that she understood the value of my magick and my connection with Genny, who I'd been missing dearly. The otter rested next to my feet in our treehouse, which I had to carry her up to and down from several times a day. We'd have to figure out a solution for that if we remained in Yannava, which I hoped we would. There was no way a sea otter, not even a magickal one, could learn to scale a tree. Perhaps a basket with a pulley? I could see myself putting Evren in such a contraption if Mycel let me. "Wow, that feels strange to say out loud," she added under her breath.

"Throne. Son," I mused aloud. "It's all very foreign. But I know… we danced the night away, and then Evren came right after." That night, less than a week prior, had been one of the happiest and most hopeful we'd had in a very long time. I prayed to never lose the memory of Mycel dancing freely with her people and friends, of the warmth that we all felt gathered around a table full of food, and the way that Mycel had fallen into my arms at the end of the night, exhausted but pleased. She radiated excitement and hope; it had been such a leap of faith to share her most vulnerable memories with the entirety of Yannava, but it had been her truth and a display of her devotion to her people. Soon, I'd likely forget the fatigue of the journey but not the loss involved in getting to that point. We had traveled far and recruited many allies, all to get back into the kingdom of Yannava. That wasn't even the fight! The thought alone felt a bit defeatist if I dwelled on it for too long. Better to recall the way Mycel's cheeks had been flushed pink as she laughed and told me all about her homeland.

"This is the clearing they say I was born in," she told me in the dark of the forest evening, while the merriment of her people filled the air of the woods. She chuckled, then snorted a little. "'They' makes it sound like a legend, like it's something my people have told their kids about throughout centuries of Yannavi history. Really, it's just my aunts, right?"

"Is that so?"

"Mmhmm, it is! And Maz was hatched from an egg on that very same day." She giggled, then pulled me in for a kiss. I wondered if our son was rolling joyfully within her belly, reacting to all of the new foods and sensations he'd experienced that evening. Mycel had the bubbly, bright energy of a forest nymph. Perhaps she was reverting back to her true form now that she was in her homeland, amongst her people. Her elation was contagious.

"Then this is the best spot in the world, I'd say," I told her, tangling my fingers into hers so that she wouldn't skip off too far in the dark. Sometimes it felt like she'd just run off and become part of the forest if I didn't hold on to her tight enough. "Stay here with me, I want to appreciate it a bit." The clearing was calm and cool and felt reflective of my mood; there was something peaceful and comforting about where the day had ended, despite knowing the pure chaos that was undoubtedly around the corner. The air shifted lightly; a cool breeze and the vibrating energy of the forest's inhabitants caused it to buzz. I may have been imagining it, but it felt like there was something special at play there, some air of magick that was special to that specific spot. I breathed in deep, savoring the unique energy of the ground we were standing on, and wondered a bit how being born from the earth really worked. If anyone had popped out of a giant mushroom rather than a womb, it was Mycel. "A spot where the greatest magick lives and creates… and where my favorite person was born."

Mycel smiled at me, then reached a slender hand up to tangle in my hair. She seemed drunk on her excitement. I'd had a few glasses of Reed's birch wine myself, but often found I couldn't keep up with the buzz of Mycel's natural vigor. She vibrated on a different level than I did, than most people did, and I wondered who our son would take after. "I'm your favorite?" Her tone was flirtatious, as if we had just met and weren't instead married with a child on the way and an entire kingdom ready to charge into battle under our command. I appreciated the levity of her attitude; she seemed younger, almost childish, in her silliness and it was a side of her that I hadn't seen in a long time. Who could blame her for succumbing to the weight of all she'd been through? It wasn't as though I had ever had such a silly and carefree side, at least not that I could recall; I had always been dark and heavy in comparison.

I chuckled. "You already knew that, Mycel of Yannava." I gave her hand a soft squeeze and admired the twinkle of her eyes.

"And what about when this baby comes?" Her gaze had been sparkly in the moonlight, as if it intended to put me in a trance. She could've done that without tricks. I was at Mycel's mercy then and always. A single word could fell me, and it often did, especially if it was "Earwyn" or "please" or "come."

"I'll love him, of course," I assured her, searching her gaze to try to understand her question. I feared it might not be as quickly as his mother would, but I knew that anything that came from our love would be easy to attach myself to. "But you and I came first. We're his foundation; he needs us to be strong together." My parents had had a similar mindset, of course, but they went about it all wrong, in my eyes. They had prioritized their well-being and comfort, their luxuries, over my basic needs. Instead, Mycel and I would value our union in order to best provide for our son; I knew that in my heart without even having to address it aloud. We were nothing like my parents. I had no fear of becoming like them because I knew that we could never be so harsh or cruel… that we operated in love and trust. That was enough to make all the difference.

My wife's eyes grew misty, and I doubted my comments; had I upset her by not focusing enough on the baby? He was important, sure, but… "You're creating a good family, Earwyn. Loyal and peaceful and loving. You're going to be a good father. I'm glad that…" She paused and swallowed hard, as if she were fighting back tears. She hadn't really been extra emotional during her pregnancy, but the past forty-eight hours had felt like the culmination of a lot of hard work, and I couldn't blame her for feeling whatever she was feeling in that moment. "I'm glad that you survived every hurdle that life has thrown at you, so that you could end up here, with us."

The acknowledgement cut deep into me, exposing my most vulnerable parts and leaving me feeling raw, like Mycel often did. To have her recognize that life had time and time again attempted to still my heart, but that I'd kept fighting because I believed there was a purpose, a person, waiting for me somewhere… My breath caught in my throat at her words, as if she could see right through me, read through my mind. It almost hurt to keep looking at her, so I slid a hand into her tawny locks and pulled her to me, crushing her lips against mine. She tasted like cranberry jam and pine. When she traced her hands down my chest, my heartbeat hammering against her fingers, then lowered herself to her knees in front of me, I bit my lip so hard it hurt. "Mycel, what are you—"

"I want you," she said coolly, as if it were obvious. The carefree, childish Mycel was gone and had quickly been replaced by a version with bold intensity.

"You have me, anytime, anywhere, but I don't know that the forest floor at nine months pregnant is the best—"

"You just said anytime, anywhere…" Her gaze was mischievous.

She didn't wait for my reply before unlacing my trousers and letting them slide to the forest floor. I couldn't find the words to respond anyway, so I suppose it didn't really matter. Before rational thought returned to my mind, she'd pulled my boxers down and was stroking me while staring up at me with all the love in the world in her gaze. Her eyes, portals to the very forest she was birthed from, glittered in the moonlight. "Is now an option?"

"Y-yes, of course," I forced out, struggling to find words between my already quickening breaths. It would never not be exciting to be touched by her. "But you really don't…" I couldn't help but feel like I should be kneeling before her, the new queen of Yannava, especially when she was so pregnant and probably so exhausted, but when I tried to pull her up to me, she seemed to be spurred on. She clicked her tongue at me in chastisement and then took me between her lips, so plush and warm, enveloping my cock. I throbbed in her mouth, and she hummed in delight. Time and time again, Mycel reminded me how good intimacy could feel, despite having feared it for so long. I tangled my fingers in her tawny mane, which was wild and no doubt had a few twigs in it. I longed to compliment her eloquently, but in those moments it was a wonder I could put two words together into a cohesive thought. "So good…" was all I could grunt out as I tried to keep my wits about me and failed.

Her gaze met mine again, the moonlight twinkling in its reflection. I always wanted her, but right then I was desperate for her. I wanted to devour her, to have her so close to me that we became one, and I groaned louder than expected when my cock hit the back of her throat. "You're beautiful," I told her, stroking her cheek as she continued to slide me in and out of her mouth. Meanwhile, she stroked me with one hand while the other gripped my thigh so that she could steady herself. "And far too good at that," I continued, "but I need you closer." I pulled her upright so that we were face-to-face and stifled a gasp as my spit-slicked cock hit the cool night air.

"How close?"

I laughed a little, forever amused by the small talk that went into intimacy and certain that I would always struggle with it. Somehow her comments were always flawless, only making me harder, while I… "I need you to bounce on my cock," I told her finally before planting a soft kiss on her lips, where the taste of me lingered.

"Are you sure you can swing that?" she retorted, smiling against my mouth. "There's a lot more of me now than there has been in the past." Without looking down, I could tell she was gesturing to her belly.

"You wound me," I told her with a laugh before hoisting her into my arms. I knew she was referring to the fact that her pregnant self took up a bit more space than her non-pregnant body did, but I wasn't fazed. "Are you questioning my strength? I may not have magick, but nothing's going to stop me from making love to my wife," I told her. It took a moment, but I managed to work her panties off and hike her dress up around her waist, ignoring the fact that I'd likely torn in it in the process. I gripped her ass roughly and snuck a finger between her thighs to caress the damp slit of her pussy, which elicited a soft whimper and giggle from her. I couldn't have been any harder. I was straining, precome dripping from the head of my cock already. I thought I might explode the second we made contact again, but I needed her. "Ready for me?"

"Mmm, yes," she purred, wiggling against my hands as if to close the gap between us.

I bit my lip hard, trying to divert some of my focus away from the divine sensations that were likely going to send me over the edge faster than I liked… and when I lowered Mycel onto my cock, her head fell back in pleasure. Goosebumps scattered across my flesh. Hell, she gripped me like a vise. I thrusted up into her once, twice, then found my rhythm before I pressed my lips against her sweat-slicked throat. "You take me so well, goddess," I told her.

"How many times can I make you come before you're too tired to go on?"

Mycel laughed playfully. "Should we make a bet?" Her humorous side vanished, however, when I switched angles a bit and caused her to gasp. "Oh!" She was drenched, and I felt her wetness slicking the space between us. I wanted to feel her dripping down my balls.

"There?" I asked, my voice low and gravelly, so different that it almost took me by surprise. I pressed my mouth against her throat, trailing kisses across her flesh and savoring the taste of her sweat. "Tell me."

"There, there," she said through gasping breaths as we chased her first orgasm. She pulled me up from her neck and kissed me hard, like the pull of her own climax was so overwhelming that she needed me to dive into it with her. "Oh, oh, god, Earwyn, right there!" When she came, shivering and whimpering into my mouth, I couldn't help but smile.

"Again," I demanded, delighting in the way her pussy rippled around my prick with the aftershock of her climax. She'd be milking me dry in no time.

She laughed again, and I throbbed inside of her, the sound music to my ears. A happy Mycel was, in some ways, my biggest turn-on. "What's the rush? We have time…" She ran her hands down my chest, then gripped one of my pecs hard, staking her claim on me. The sensation sent a rush through every inch of my body. I was just about to reply, however, when we were interrupted.

"Mycel! Come on, we need a toast! The people are demanding a—" Reed's voice cut through the thick forest air, but of course he halted in his tracks when he realized what he was interrupting. His mouth hung open, but I barely caught a glimpse of it because he promptly turned and left.

"Maybe not as much time as I thought," Mycel added, her cheeks suddenly more flushed than they were before. How did she feel having her ex-lover catch her like this? Was she embarrassed? She'd told me she couldn't be more mine, what with our marriage and child, but something in me felt the primal urge to claim her more in that moment.

"At least once more then," I insisted and gripped her thighs a little tighter. "We have time for that. Make time for that."

She whimpered, undoubtedly sensitive from her first orgasm and still coming down, her thighs trembling around my waist. "But I just…"

A bit of jealousy and the primal need to claim her again and again overcame me. I didn't care if she was late for her toast, didn't care who heard her come repeatedly, didn't care how Reed of Yannava felt. I withdrew from her, and she gasped, the cold air hitting both of us in a rush. "He won't interrupt again," I grunted, laying her down in the clearing, despite the frigid air. The heat from our bodies would easily melt the gathering frost, and I was prepared to lose a limb to frostbite then if it meant accomplishing my goals. Mycel, on the other hand, could likely never be harmed by the forest. I loomed over her, taking in her soft, pale face in the moonlight. Her cheeks were bright pink, her hair in a chaotic halo around her. She looked surprised. "My wife. My queen," I told her seriously. "Mine to please."

"Never a doubt," she replied, a playful smile replacing her shock. "Oh?"

My wife then reached between us, snaking a hand past her pregnant belly to grip my cock. I followed her lead, sliding into her again, and marveled at how soft and tight she was. I wondered if pregnancy had made her extra sensitive, too. "So please me," she said finally, challenging me with her stare.

I thrust into her languidly at first, propping myself up on my knees so that I could hike her legs up, spreading her wide. "Don't worry, I'll be prepared to carry you back when we're done."

"Carry me, Wonder?"

Each time I thrust into her deeper, my balls heavy and aching as they slapped against her ass. "Yes," I grunted. I reached a hand between us and brushed my thumb over her clit, savoring the way a shudder ran through her body instantly. "I don't imagine you'll be able to walk after this."

The look on her face was one I had not seen before in this setting: overwhelming pleasure mixed with disbelief, with surprise, almost as if she was afraid to let herself tip over the edge. "That's it, baby," I told her, maintaining my rhythm and savoring each desperate whimper I was fucking out of her.

"Wyn, it's too much— I—"

"I've got you, let go."

Her breaths came in frantic gusts. Her back arched. And she screamed out into the biting cold of winter, "Earwyn!" I was shocked, too, when a gush of warmth left her at her climax, drenching my cock and balls. I leaned over to scoop her into my arms as she came and let her ride out her orgasm on my lap, where she continued to tremble and twitch until she was boneless in my arms. Within seconds the ground rumbled with life that didn't belong in the wintering forest, sprouts of flowers pushing through the hardened dirt.

Mine to please.

Mine to take places she'd never been before.

"Mine."

* * *

I must have been smiling to myself as I recalled the encounter because Mycel had a peculiar look on her face when she caught my gaze again. "What's on your mind?" she asked, her tone more serious now that my magick was on the line.

"You," I said with a laugh. "Almost always." Before I could elaborate, she pressed a kiss to my lips that made my heart race.

Some small part of me was nervous to be reunited with my magick; it had been gone for so long that I almost understood what it was like to be human, to be fully mortal. I hated it. Not only did I feel more on edge than ever with my vulnerability at such a peak level, but I felt disconnected from the earth, as if I were in a daze. I'd need that connection if I was going to be useful – and alive – for the duration of whatever battles were heading our way and for the life that would hopefully carry on long after the last sword fell. I needed my magick to exist in this world with my wife and our son. Genny looked up at me from her spot on the treehouse floor, and I could tell that she, too, was missing our connection.

Mycel, meanwhile, looked nervous. "I've never done this before."

"Me neither," I told her with a shrug.

"That happens a lot with us, don't you think?"

"There's no one I'd rather try new things with," I told her. "Outside, perhaps?" I wasn't sure what my rationale was, but if this was about reconnection with the earth, I figured the closer to it, the better. I scooped up Genny, and we left Evren asleep in his crib with Maz watching dutifully over him. We'd only be a few feet below him if we left the treehouse to stand on the ground. I didn't miss Mycel's longing glance as she followed me down, however. "He's safe."

She was silent as we descended the ladder, and once we were firmly on the forest floor, she looked at me with a soft sadness in her eyes. "I didn't expect it to be so... intense."

"What do you mean?"

My wife glanced up at the treehouse, longing apparent in her gaze. "I've always felt things... acutely, but this is a lot. The second I laid eyes on him, it felt like the entire world had shifted around me, like everything became deeper, stronger, brighter, and darker at the same time."

"Sounds like when I first saw you," I told her, tucking a strand of hair behind her ear. I leaned forward and planted a kiss on her newly exposed cheek. It was different for each of us, I think; I already loved Evren, but I didn't have the same bond that Mycel had with him. She would always come first to me. "Every sense amplified…"

She smiled, and the heavens may as well have parted in that moment. When she leaned forward into my arms and wrapped hers around my waist, I rested my cheek on top of her head. "Let me ride those waves with you, no matter how turbulent they get, okay?" Ocean metaphors… how appropriate.

"Yeah…" Then she kissed me again, soft and sweet, the taste of her lips like fresh berries and honey. The mother of my child. The keeper of my heart. The queen of my universe. "Let's get your magick back."

"I'm ready."

CHAPTER FOUR

MYCEL

 $\mathcal{I}$ wasn't ready. I had no clue what I was doing. There were plenty of things I knew how to do with magick and some I had dug deep into my connection with the earth to try – like Ossian and Tana's fertility ritual, the success of which I still had not heard back about. But removing and reinstating magick, let alone magick outside of my domain and element, was the work of a ruler, a role in which I had not fully settled. There was no manual for being the ruler of a terrafolk kingdom. You would think that all things magickal would be intuitive, but they aren't, and I had no idea where to begin when it came to getting my husband his magick back. This was going to be a problem.

I couldn't blame Earwyn for his impatience when he said again, "I'm ready, goddess." That same eagerness and urgency and desperate longing had filled me when I'd been separated from my own magick and from Maz. With everything that Earwyn had endured, I knew that reconnecting with that part of his soul would be grounding, a step toward healing. He needed this. I needed to figure this out for him.

"Earwyn…" I bit my lip, avoiding his gaze.

"What is it?" My husband looked like he was trying to hide his concern.

"I don't even know where to begin." I was starting to panic internally, partially because I had no idea what to do but also because I'd been away from Evren for several minutes now. My brain felt like it was trying to run in two different directions; I fought my desperate instinct to call up to Maz for an update on Evren and tried to focus on my husband before me.

That same ferocity from the treehouse flashed in his gaze again. I couldn't place it; I didn't feel unsafe, but I expected that there was a very dangerous part of my man bubbling beneath the surface. It was the same part of him that had jumped magick-less into the ocean to slaughter the liopleurodon. There was, undoubtedly, a feral side of Earwyn. "Can you try?"

"Yes," I told him. "Of course. But if it doesn't work, we'll figure out what to do. I can think of a few people who might know the answer." Hesitantly, I placed my hands on the sides of Earwyn's neck, where his gills had long since scabbed and scarred over since his return to earthside. When he'd been taken from me, they'd torn open and bled profusely. I remembered his screams of agony so vividly and the way it had felt when my own gills had ripped their way through my flesh back in Seattle. Would that happen again? Was there a peaceful way to transition? Then, I pressed my forehead to his and closed my eyes, breathing deeply to center myself. I didn't have the same water magick anymore; that had transferred solely to Evren upon his birth, but my connection to the forest and to Yannava felt stronger than ever. Earwyn leaned into my touch, and our breathing synchronized: a moment of connection I didn't realize I'd been missing. I could do this, I had to do this. My husband's well-being depended on it.

The sound of the trees swaying in the cool winter air filled my ears. Maz chittering to a sleeping baby Evren: *Is he breathing? Yep, he's breathing. How about now? Okay, good.* The crunch of the frozen ground beneath boots and bare feet. Creatures rolling sleepily in their caves. Plants sleeping soundly beneath the dirt, awaiting the reliable warmth of spring to wake once again.

"Do you feel that?"

"The earth, yes," Earwyn said, voice low as he homed in on the shifting nature around him.

I focused hard and tried to pick out the sounds of water from my mind. A lazy stream. Rocks shifting with the flow of water. Far off, the ocean crashing against the shore, frigid and powerful; despite its lazy demeanor, it can be deadly. It reminded me a lot of a bear with its dopey and uncoordinated appearance that could turn threatening in an instant.

"And the sea."

Come on, I thought. *There has to be some sort of incantation for this.*

Like magick words? Maz commented from up in the treehouse. *He's still breathing, by the way... and... yep, still breathing.*

Yes, I thought to Maz. *Do you know of anything?*

Um, no.

I groaned internally, trying not to let my frustration show to Earwyn, and mustered up the closest thing I could. Magick words. Come on. *Dear forest, please return Earwyn's magick... to its... rightful... I don't know, come on, give him his magick back, please!*

When I opened my eyes again, I came face-to-face with Earwyn's unimpressed stare. "Did it work?"

"No," he said, not accusing or disappointed, just matter-of-fact, though I knew that he must be disappointed inside. I would have been. "But you're holding me captive again."

I followed his gaze to his legs, where vines had wound themselves over his pants and mine, pulling us together like green rope. I dismissed them with a flick of my wrist, then looked at my husband sheepishly. "Sorry."

"It's okay, my love."

"I need to go talk to Hyssop," I told Earwyn, feeling defeated at that admission. "She'll know how to get it back."

"Isn't there anyone else?" Earwyn leaned down to brush his pants off.

I shook my head. "I don't think so. I doubt Clove had anything to do with me losing my magick, so it must have been Hyssop. Either that, or I can ask Reed if he has any memories with—"

"Perhaps not," Earwyn suggested a little more quickly than I had anticipated. "He seemed to be somewhere else the last time we saw him. A lot on his mind, maybe?"

* * *

THE HOLDING CELLS OF YANNAVA WERE NOTHING LIKE THE ONES THAT Earwyn and I had been imprisoned in at Ulmos. Of course, there were the very obvious differences; one was built of rusted metal, worn away by seawater, and ours consisted of cells made of wood, bound by vines, enchanted to nullify the magick of anyone inside them, though as queen I was immune to that particular enchantment. I also had a sneaking suspicion that we were slightly more hospitable to our prisoners than the Ulmosi, though Earwyn and I hadn't stayed in Ulmos long enough to find out what, if anything, they were going to feed us prior to our planned execution. Perhaps they had planned to throw us some rotting fish before we were marched out to the shark tank for Rhodes to eat us. Also unlike Ulmos, our holding cells were few, and only one remained inhabited. As I approached the cell I had come for, I realized that we would have to move Hyssop soon. The cells were directly on the ground level; without being relocated, she would drown.

The guards, likely some of the same that had turned me away at the entrance of the city months ago, bowed their heads in respect as they let me through. It felt odd, and I couldn't help the quiet "thanks" that slipped from my mouth as I passed them. Yep, thanks, thanks for not killing me or threatening to kill me this time. Good job, much appreciated. Despite my lingering bitterness, I could see their point of view.

As if she could read my mind, Hyssop immediately chimed in. "You're thanking them? They work for you."

I groaned internally and rolled my eyes like a petulant child who was sick of her mother's snide commentary. Part of me wished that Hyssop could experience the bleak dilapidation of the Ulmosi dungeons. "Is this really how we're going to begin this interaction?"

"It just solidifies my stance; you are not ready to lead these people to safety. It would be better for everyone if they turned you over." Again, I had just arrived, and she was jumping right into her verbal attacks.

Her words cut deep. How could they not? This woman had raised me from a little mushroom spore, and yet, here she was, praying for my demise. I swallowed hard. I wanted to believe that my aunt, the one who loved me, was in there somewhere… "How can you say such a thing? Has all of this been worth the loss of your people and your family? I know you don't care about me, but what about Clove?"

Hyssop scoffed. Her normally perfectly coiffed hairstyle had come apart with her imprisonment, and a few strands fell to one side of her face as she shook her head. I had never seen her so disheveled. Knowing her, it was driving her a little bit mad, too. "Clove is delusional. I've tried to get her to see clearly, but she's living a lie."

"And your grandnephew?"

"Now that," Hyssop replied, a far-off look in her eyes as if she were deep in some great, horrible vision, "is a different story. My grandnephew has the ability to change the fate of our people. I don't think you realize how valuable it is to have an heir to both kingdoms' thrones within our grasp…"

I scowled. "Within your grasp? Just a tool to use, you mean." Rage bubbled in my veins at the mention of my child being used to further her agenda. He was safe, I told myself, home with Earwyn and Maz and Clove. No harm could come to him there. Still, my heart raced, and I had to fight against the intrusive images that flashed in my mind. "This isn't you." *Something is wrong here,* I told myself, certain again that this was not the type of change good people went through. Sure, momentary lapses in judgment, but to completely change one's view on the value of life and family? It seemed unlikely; it had to be due to an outside influence. "But it doesn't matter because I'm not here to talk about your stance on the war. I'm here because I know you were the one who took my magick, and I need to know how to get Earwyn's back."

Hyssop laughed. I wasn't sure if her laughter had always sounded like this – a harsh, wet cackle – but it made my skin crawl.

The longer I spent away from my family, my real family, the more uncomfortable I became. Talking to Hyssop felt like a trap. "I don't have time for this."

The soldiers that had been guarding the prison entry moved closer behind me as if to emphasize my point, but I put a hand up. "I appreciate it, but I can handle this for now. I won't hesitate to call you in if needed."

"What, are you going to torture it out of me?"

I gritted my teeth before responding. "You say that as if you hadn't been ready to hand me over to be killed. Murder, torture… What's the difference to you? I don't want to, but when it comes to the safety of my family and my people, I'm learning that I am willing to do many unpleasant things." I thought back to the blade in my boot, my trusty sidekick for so many decades, and considered whether I had the gall to use it against someone I'd once treated like a mother. Could I draw blood from one of my own, intentionally harm them in order to protect and serve the others? This felt like a very gray place to be… family had always been the ultimate good for me, the thing I was most motivated to fight for. But now, my mind was pushing back at the very thought of harming Hyssop, even if she had blatantly betrayed us on several counts. What made her different from Anala, I wondered, when I had no qualms about labeling her as the enemy?

Hyssop scoffed, as if she could hear my inner turmoil, and folded her thin arms across her chest. "You don't have it in you. Not long ago you couldn't even face your people, now you're – what – going to threaten your own aunt for them? Doubtful."

I sucked my teeth in irritation. "Strange, what we're willing to do when we're forced to pick sides, isn't it? I didn't think you were capable of turning against your wife, but here we are."

"She's on the wrong side." Hyssop's arms remained folded across her chest, her chin held high despite her haggard appearance.

"We'll see about that."

My aunt sneered. "Magick or not, it won't be enough for you to come out of this victorious. They will win head-on, or you'll run like you did last time and leave our people to perish."

"*My* people," I said confidently. The Yannavi were no longer hers… nor was I. I waited in silence, making it clear that I was done with our discussion, until she provided the steps necessary for reuniting my husband with his magick. Moments ticked by as we faced each other through the magickal bonds of Yannava's prison, and my irritation grew toward this woman who was not only putting a dent in my progress but keeping me away from my son for so long that my chest began to ache. I was fuming when I finally called for one of the guards. "Let me in." Sure, I could make quick work of her with the barrier between us, especially since she had been stripped of her power, but something dark and terrible was brewing within me… and it wanted to see my aunt close up when I finally broke her.

"I don't mean to question you, my lady, but are you sure you want to go in there… and on your own, no less?" The guard eyed Hyssop with disdain. When I nodded, he didn't argue and instead locked the cell behind me, then stood by.

Hyssop laughed, but the sudden flash of fear in her gaze was unmistakable; she was beginning to worry. And for a moment, I did too; I thought of the intimate moments I had shared with this person, how she'd held my tiny hands and taught me things, and how I imagined that she would always be a safe haven for me. Now that was gone, and all that was left was hurt, betrayal, and the opportunity to ensure that I would come out of this war alive and well, so that I could be a safe place for my own child. I leaned back against the bars of the cell long enough to dislodge the blade from my boot. "This is your last chance to cooperate and begin to mend what you've broken so carelessly."

"You got used to being without your magick," she suggested. Hyssop eyed the blade in my hand.

"This calls for a more personal approach than simply sapping the oxygen from your cell or having Maz peck at your eyes, don't you think? If I'm going to 'torture it out of you,' I'd like to do it right." I twirled the blade between the fingers of one hand. "I assume your attempt at a joke means that you won't willingly provide the information I'm looking for." When she did not reply, I crooked a finger at her, and the vines surrounding the cell immediately lashed around her ankles. Within seconds, they'd strung her upside down before me, her arms and legs bound tightly as she struggled against her green captors. Another gesture, and they pulled her up higher so that we were face-to-face, her intricate hairdo coming fully undone thanks to gravity, and her prominent cheekbones now graced with flushed pink flesh. "After all, weren't you the one who accused me of running from my problems? I'm staring one in the eyes right now."

"You can't scare me," Hyssop grunted, shifting against her bonds. The way her breathing grew shallow and panicked suggested otherwise.

I closed a fist in the air, and the vines tightened around her more, restricting her movement and consequently, her ability to breathe. Still, she fought back. "If you kill me," she said with a wheeze, "then who will tell you – how to get his magick back? – Clove doesn't know – or she would've told you already."

"You won't let me kill you," I retorted. "No one that is this invested in the war cares so little about their life. It's just a matter of how much you'll let me hurt you before you finally give in."

She fought and struggled, and the vines tightened again until she was gasping for breath. Though it didn't stop me, the sight made me incomprehensibly uncomfortable. When she finally fainted, I found that I wasn't really sure how to torture someone. I let the vines loosen and patted her cheek, trying to rouse her. It didn't work, so I laid a hand across her face in the slap I'd been aching to deal her since I learned about her betrayal, and she gasped awake. "Stay with me, auntie," I told her. "Next time it might take me longer to loosen these up," I said, tapping on the vines around her midsection. "And then who knows what'll happen." Even I was shocked at my callous approach.

I fiddled with the blade again, unsure of how I'd use it when its primary purpose had been cutting up fruit or hunting for so long.

"I won't help you," she bit out, glaring at me through now glazed-over eyes.

Without thinking, I grabbed her hair, yanking her up so that our faces were only inches apart, and snarled at her. We were so close that her breath was on my cheek. "Wrong answer." I wanted to go home.

"You can hurt me. I'll heal. It'll be worth the advantage."

I knew she was right, so I did the only thing I could think wouldn't be worth the advantage to her. With my fingers tangled in a fistful of hair, I began cutting away one of Hyssop's most valued possessions. She didn't realize what was happening until the first few locks fluttered to the floor, landing in a small pile beneath her.

"I'll take it all," I told her through teeth gritted so hard that my jaw ached. "I'll call for a razor and shave your head to the skin if I need to." Then, I lied, but only because I knew it would cut her deep. "Then no one will find you beautiful, and the Ulmosi will have as little respect for you as they did their own prince. You think they'll care about your loyalty or sacrifice then? Think they'll save you a spot in their throne room when you look like every other commoner scum? We both know your hair grows slower than the draping moss of the forest; they won't wait." My heart pounded in my chest as I threatened her; I felt like a child who had disobeyed their parents in a bout of overconfidence, just waiting for the repercussions of their actions. It was terrifying to feel so small, so young and fragile, even when I had the upper hand. I tried to calm myself and without thinking, fell into humming a tune from my childhood as I snipped away more and more hair. "Remember this?" I asked before humming another verse of a song the words of which I had long forgotten; all I could remember was that it was about a seed growing into a plant. "You used to sing it to me when you brushed my hair…"

The way she trembled at my words told me that I'd finally struck a chord. I stifled a sigh of relief, knowing that this was the last weapon I had in my arsenal and that Hyssop, more than anyone, was capable of withstanding a lot to get her way… perhaps that was where I'd gotten the trait from. Threatening something as valuable to her as her hair when I knew that my husband had the same connection to his hurt me more than I'd expected… and was it her hair or some tiny, sentimental connection to the song that had finally done her in? Was there a heart, a whisper of love for me, in that hollow shell somewhere? I loosened the vines once more and kept my gaze on my aunt. "Tell me, now."

Hyssop closed her eyes, almost as if it were too painful to admit defeat. Perhaps she feared for her safety if the Ulmosi discovered that she'd surrendered this information to us. "As long as he's still considered Ulmosi, they'll continue to have control over his magick."

I didn't know what the hell that meant for us, but I trusted that it was all the information Hyssop had. The threat had gotten to her, and rather than show my uncertainty, I turned on my heel and ordered the guard to release me. "Cut her down, please."

* * *

WHEN I RETURNED TO EARWYN, HE WAS BACK UP IN THE TREEHOUSE with a very fussy Evren Firth, who apparently was desperate to nurse. It took everything in me not to snatch the baby from my husband's arms, and I fought the urge because I knew that it would leave Earwyn feeling as strange as I did. The way I couldn't really breathe until I had the baby pressed against me again was outlandish, and frankly, it frightened me; I knew that soon, sooner than I liked, Evren Firth would be locked away somewhere with the rest of our city's fragile people, while his father and I fought to protect the Yannavi. I told myself those thoughts would have to wait; there were, unfortunately, more pressing matters at hand. As I sat in my usual spot by the window of our home, Evren finally content and us co-regulated, I mulled over the information Hyssop had given me. It wasn't much… just a few sentences that I repeated in my head over and over, as if that repetition would bring me clarity.

Earwyn looked concerned: a common expression when it came to his feelings toward me. He sat on the side of our bed, facing my chair, and ran a hand through his sandy mane. "What is it? The fact that you haven't told me yet has me worried it's something insane."

I was fiddling with my wedding ring when I realized what she'd meant. In the end, there was really only one way to take what she'd told me. "Not insane," I murmured, glancing at Earwyn's hands. If I stared too long, I could get caught up in just how much I loved them; his skin was soft, but his touch was always firm, certain, and assuring.

His once-bronze flesh was now a bit paler due to his time away from the sun. "Just not ideal for being in the middle of war preparations."

"I'm listening…" His tone was patient, but I knew that he must be dying inside to hear the full story.

"You've got to be part of the Yannavi in order for their leader – me – to have any control over your magick. Right now the Ulmosi still have rule over you, which is why your magick is still compromised; they're obviously not going to reinstate it while you're running from them."

He scowled at the mention of his former home. "Aren't I part of the Yannavi, though? We're married." Earwyn held up his left hand, where my replacement ring caught a ray of winter light and shined happily, as if to say *Don't forget about me!*

Warmth bloomed in my chest at the sight; I'd poured every ounce of love and longing I had into that replacement ring, and I knew he'd never let it go. I smiled a little, recalling our wedding in the woods, which had been blissful and perfect, up until it wasn't. "I don't know that the forest recognizes our union yet."

Anyone else would've rolled their eyes, but Earwyn simply looked at me with the eagerness he always had toward my ideas. "What are you proposing?"

"Another wedding, an official one… here, in Yannava. If it's offici-ated by my people and we're surrounded by them, there's no way it can be disputed that you're one of us and…"

Earwyn raised an eyebrow.

"And, well, the king of the woods."

He laughed at the title. Whether it was the preposterousness of suggesting that someone could truly be the king of all of the woods, the fact that he probably didn't feel ready, or the suggestion that he'd have any interest in being royalty again, I couldn't tell. "Um, are you sure you want to marry me *again*?" he asked finally.

I couldn't help the snort that came out with my amused chuckle.

"You mean, am I sure I want to marry the man of my dreams and the father of my child? Yeah, I think I could go for that twice… Besides, it would be nice to have a wedding without an interruption this time." I cringed internally at the memory of him being dragged into the water by an Ulmosi guard; the memory seemed like a million years ago, but had left a wound in my heart that still hadn't fully healed. "What do you say, Wonder?"

"Well, since I didn't get the chance last time, and we're doing everything officially now," Earwyn mused aloud before lowering himself onto one knee and taking my hand into his. "Mycel, would you do me the immense honor of securing our union in front of your people and marry me again?"

Warmth bloomed in my chest, and I was moved more than I expected; I'd never regretted being the one to ask him to marry me, but there was something different about him asking. "Yes, a million times, yes."

CHAPTER FIVE

EARWYN

*M*uch like the celebration of Mycel's coronation, our wedding brought much needed joy and levity to the forest during a time that was otherwise heavy with fear of the unknown. Aside from a couple of curious questions – mainly "why now?" – most of the Yannavi were ecstatic at the idea of banding together for something positive; like Mycel, they were bright and joyous people who valued community and closeness. Since my former people were closing in on us, as evidenced by the flooding forest, it felt necessary to attempt this.

The promise of returning my magick was so close... part of me worried it wouldn't work and that the wedding would appear to be a selfish event for our own sakes. But if it did work – and I needed it to work – I felt confident that it would be worth it. Mortal me was near useless. I could swim, sure, and I was a strong enough person by human standards, but without magick I worried about my ability to contribute in a fight. I needed to be able to protect Mycel and our son and our friends. I couldn't do that if I was struck down by a weapon

or the opposition's own magickal abilities, and the clock was ticking…
so the wedding was set for the next day.

That night, we muddled about with preparations as well as we
could from the treehouse, where Evren slept sprawled out in the
middle of our bed. It felt like our son had just been born, and yet he
was growing faster than I'd anticipated, changing by the day. Each
morning I awoke to a child who looked slightly older, his body more
filled out, his face less squished like it had been in his mother's belly.
In some ways, it frightened me; we were losing so much time to war,
and with everything going on, I worried that I was missing crucial
parts of my child's life. Would he be an entirely new person when all
was said and done? Would I be around to see him continue to grow?
Perhaps one day he'd be as tall as I was. I lay down on the bed next to
him, careful not to shift the mattress too much, and looked up at the
ceiling of the treehouse with a sigh. It was then that I realized this
small being would one day have his own interests and aspirations: he
would love people, he would have stories to tell and adventures to go
on… and suddenly the idea that I might not be around to support him
in all of that, to learn about the person he would become, terrified me.
But I couldn't dwell on what-ifs or the far future for too long. The
present was demanding my attention. I tucked my finger into the
palm of his tiny hand, and he squeezed it in his sleep. Then, I
wondered aloud to my wife, "Are you going to ask Zara to be your
maid of honor?"

"What does that mean?" Mycel asked, cocking her head to the side
as she paused her task of looking through clothing. Her people had
blessed her with several outfits, and she seemed determined to find
one that would work for a wedding; there wasn't time to create something from scratch, and we both knew that there was more to this ceremony than our attire. She held up a simple cream-colored dress, long-
sleeved with a V-neckline. *I might like to peel that from her flesh with my
teeth*, I thought. "She's not a maid."

I couldn't help but smile. "It's a human thing. Brides usually pick their favorite, uh, friend to stand by their side at the altar." I'd been to a few human weddings during my time earthside, mainly for human employees of the Salt and Earth Alliance and other acquaintances who had invited me solely as a formality. It was strange to think back on my time in a suit, parading around as a businessman. It felt foreign, like a past life; I had been charismatic, outgoing, and self-assured back then, none of which I felt anymore. "Surprisingly, it doesn't have anything to do with the type of maid you're thinking of."

"And the groom?" I hadn't thought of that when I made the suggestion, and apparently neither had Mycel, because she immediately clasped a hand over her mouth. Her eyebrows knitted immediately with regret. "I'm so sorry. Sorry," she said through her fingers, her voice barely above a whisper. Having Firth by my side would have meant the world, of course, but aside from him I didn't have many options. Who would I ask? Rhodes? Reed?! My stomach turned at the thought, but then I realized that Reed had made himself scarce since the baby was born… Whatever his reasoning, it was nice to have less Reed in my life. As the Yannavi historian, however, he would undoubtedly be present at the wedding itself.

"It's okay." I rose from the bed, eyeing my son to ensure he didn't roll off when I got up. Genny must have read my mind, even without our usual connection, because she climbed up onto the bed using a chest at the foot of it, and curled up next to Evren, blocking him from the edge of the bed. I closed the distance between Mycel and myself, then moved her hand from her lips and pressed it to mine. "You should ask Zara, though. I think it would mean a lot to her."

CHAPTER SIX

ZARA

Mycel and Earwyn were getting married. Again. Part of me started to feel sorry for myself. I didn't know if Firth and I would've ever gotten married, but it would've been nice to have the option. This wasn't about me, though; my best friend was getting married! But this time I knew about it. I was having an internal battle with myself about being present for a wedding – which was supposed to happen in just a few hours – with everything going on around us, when Mycel burst into the front door of my dwelling. She'd only told me the night before, and since then I'd been stressing over my duties as a best friend: what to wear, where to sit, who to sit next to. Perhaps I was supposed to be helping with preparations otherwise, but I didn't even know many of the Yannavi's names… they hadn't really excluded me from anything so far, but it would've felt weird to just butt in to the wedding planning when I had no clue what terrafolk weddings were supposed to be like. Hell, who knew what kind of strange rituals these people had in place? It wasn't that long ago that I'd walked in on Mycel smearing wet potting soil all over her face and trying to play it off as a mud mask.

"Zara!" she exclaimed, out of breath as if she had sprinted to my dwelling. Her reddish hair fluttered around her flushed face through the open door, and a chill shot through my body; I'd only been keeping warm thanks to the tiny floating fire that Zahir had left me with.

"Sprout..." I nodded cautiously, then stepped around her to close the door once more.

"I need to talk to you."

Ah, shit. Was this whole ordeal going to be even worse than I feared? I honestly needed a break from the internal turmoil for just a second.

I folded my arms across my chest. "What is it?"

Mycel wrung the fabric of her jacket between her fingers. "I love you."

I smiled. "I know. Now spit it out."

My best friend laughed, then spun in place before flopping onto my bed. For the briefest moment, it felt like we were back in our apartment, venting after a long day or chittering about a fun date. The nostalgia filled me with warmth and longing at the same time. But even I could admit that my dwelling in Yannava was an upgrade from our dingy Seattle apartment. The bed alone was bigger and softer; back in the apartment Mycel and I had scrunched up on each other's twin-sized beds when needed. Mine had proven especially challenging for me and Firth to cuddle on. Here I could spread out and still not hit the edges of the bed... could roll around while dreaming and stay atop the plush mattress and layered comforters. It was different and lovely. Different could be nice, I was learning slowly. Things could change and be okay... not great, but okay... and neutrality was better than agony. Even though I'd associated Firth with his magickal world ever since he revealed it to me, being in Yannava was actually a lot less painful than being back at our apartment would have been. Still, I missed it terribly. I thought back to the night that Firth had given me my sign name.

"Show me again," I'd told him, trying hard not to let my smile overtake my entire face after he'd shown me the sign. My cheeks already hurt from grinning so hard, but that was often the case around Firth. I missed that.

He used my sign name once more, then pulled me into his arms and pressed his lips to mine. At first, I didn't fight it, but then I realized he hadn't answered my questions. "Wait," I muttered, pushing him away with my hands on his chest. I pulled them away only to continue signing. "When were you going to tell me?"

"When I thought it was safe. I couldn't risk putting you in harm's way, Z. I mean, you see now just how nuts everything is."

"I can take care of myself!" I folded my arms and stuck my chin up at him, pouting. I did that a lot with him.

He looked exasperated, but at the same time couldn't stop another little smirk that weaseled its way onto his face; he liked the pouting. I liked that he liked it, even in those moments of pure chaos, even when things were far too serious for us to be flirting. "I know you can. But you saw what happened to Earwyn and… and I just had to drown your best friend! No one could have predicted that, okay?" He flexed his hands, which were no doubt fatigued from holding her under the water for so long. I knew as well as anyone that Mycel was strong and that Firth, with his still-healing wounds, had to put up a good fight to keep her down. I wouldn't forget that image for a long time to come… the look on Mycel's face when she could no longer hold her breath and the way that Firth, despite his frustration with both of us, looked so pained as he held her under.

"And you! And what happened to you! Don't downplay that." I jerked a finger in the direction of his abdomen, which was still bandaged. The wound beneath had been atrocious, a festering gash that had gotten worse and worse until Mycel and I had ventured into the forest for a remedy. At one point, I was certain that the magickal wound would continue to eat away at his flesh until there was nothing left. There had been some bandage changes where chunks of flesh peeled away with his coverings, giving me a clear view of the sinewy muscle beneath. I couldn't imagine the agonizing pain he was suppressing, despite his body beginning to heal.

Firth laughed, and the sound sent a chill through my body. He was like my own personal Atlas – colossal and powerful – and I was his Earth to hold up and protect. "I've seen way worse."

"That's not funny," I signed to him, then threw my hands up. "It shouldn't be normal for you to get beat up!" If he wasn't already hurt, I'd threaten to beat him up myself.

"Babe," Firth signed, pausing only to run his hands through his short hair as he searched for a way to placate me. He needed a haircut. I wanted to cut his hair for him. "It's part of my job. Actually, it's my whole job. Protecting Earwyn, no matter the cost."

I scowled. "I hate your job. And if anything else happens to you because you're busy protecting Earwyn, I'll—"

Firth caught my hands and lowered them, then looked me in the eyes. "Nothing is going to happen to me," he said, this time speaking aloud. He spoke often, especially when we were with others, but for some reason the deep smoothness of his voice always surprised me. "We haven't had enough time together, haven't laughed together enough, okay? We have a lot more to do before I d—"

"Don't say 'die,' or I'll kill you myself!" I turned my face away from him because I was trying not to cry. I hated crying, especially around Firth. He wasn't anything but gentle and comforting, but I didn't like going to that place and needing him to pull me out. He was already tasked with protecting so many other people that it felt unfair for me to put that additional work on him.

"Babe…"

"I was so scared, Firth," I told him honestly, hating how weak it made me sound. I scrubbed my face frustratedly, wishing that the right amount of pressure would stop the tears from coming, and looked up at him. "You weren't moving. There was blood everywhere. Do you know how long you were out for? Days! The world stopped. We just took turns trying to keep you comfortable and make sure you were still breathing. I could see your insides! That's not right, Firth. Do you know how scary that is?"

"I'm sorry, Z." Firth nodded, his expression softening a bit. He was trying to brush it off, to make it seem like it wasn't a big deal, but we both knew it was. This wasn't normal. "And I'm sorry you had to tend to me for so long."

"Now you're just being ridiculous; it's not about having to take care of you! That's part of loving someone!"

"See, I knew you loved me." He grinned at me. When I stood there with my mouth open for way too long, he spoke again. "Nothing's going to happen," he told me with a sigh, realizing that I wasn't going to fall for his attempt to make things lighthearted again, then returned to signing. "I'm here, with you, and that's the only place I want to be. Nothing means more to me than the time I have with you, Z. I don't want any of it to be eaten up by you being mad at me. How can I make it up to you?"

"Take my mind off the thought of you…" I trailed off. I couldn't say it again, not even to lovingly threaten him.

Firth grabbed my hands and placed them on his chest. "I'm not going anywhere, okay? I'm right here with you, where I belong." Then, he pulled me into his arms, and I wrapped my legs around his waist, a little nervous to press against his injury but needing more than anything to feel close to him again after so long. When he kissed me, it was clear he felt the same. Looking back, there were very few things that I wouldn't do to experience that again… Before meeting Firth, I hadn't believed in soulmates, but there was just something electric about being close to him. It felt right. It felt safe. It felt easy, natural, like I was home. He was my home.

"You have too many clothes on, baby," I told him when our kiss broke, leaning down to nibble at his jawline, which was scattered with stubble from his time not shaving. I was panting already. "Take them off."

"Yes, ma'am."

It was effortful to leave that memory and come back to the real world, but I finally did. There were no memories of Firth here. He'd never slept in the bed, covered in an array of handmade blankets from Mycel's people, nor had he cooked in the tiny kitchen of my dwelling. There was no TV that we'd fallen asleep watching together. This place could be a blank slate for me.

Mycel sighed and looked at me from her spot on the bed. "Will you be my maid of honor?" When I didn't respond right away, she jumped into an explanation. "I know it's a human thing, but I hear it's important, and you're important to me… and I know we didn't tell you about the first wedding, and that wasn't right because you're my best friend, and I should've told you, but I want you to be a big part of it now… even if it's not ideal because of, you know, the end of the world and the war and everything." When the last word left her lips, she held her breath, then let out an exasperated sigh. "But only if you want to. I know it's a lot. I just want you to know that you're so important to me, and I want to celebrate you somehow. But I don't want you to feel like you're some side character in my story. You deserve your own story, too, or maybe our stories can be part of each other's… so if this too much—"

"I'd love to, Sprout."

"Really?" Mycel perked up immediately, sitting upright as she stared at me with curious eyes. They were bright green and brilliant and seemed to have increased in intensity when we arrived at

Yannava; I couldn't help but feel pleased for her being so in her element. Literally.

"Yeah, but I don't really have anything to wear."

"It's okay!" Soon she was off the bed again, pulling me into a hug so soft and deep that she lifted me off the ground. A giggle escaped my lips, and I savored the connection I'd been aching for since our arrival. "We'll find something!" she told me when she set me back down. She stood back, her hands on my shoulders, and grinned. "You know, it doesn't really matter, though. You can wear whatever you want! Let's find something warm. I just want you up there with me."

"Mmm, yeah, it'll be good."

I must've been clearly distracted because Mycel looked at me curiously. "What is it?"

"It's really silly, but I miss my clothes… and my makeup and hair dye." It felt even more ridiculous to say out loud.

"It's no sillier than having a wedding in the middle of a war," she told me finally, her tone suddenly very serious. And when she returned to my dwelling maybe half an hour later, she had a huge basket in her arms.

"What the heck is all of this?"

"Well, it's not quite the selection you'd find at the mall, but it's as close as we'll get in the woods." She plopped the basket down on the small table I'd been using for meals, doodling, and on occasion, resting my head on for a good cry, and opened it up. I sidled up to her so I could take a look inside and was amazed at the sheer amount of stuff she'd thrown together in such a short period of time. As if she could read my mind, she began taking each item out to show me. First came several jars. "Beet juice," she told me, holding up the dark red liquid to the light. "Lots of Yannavi use different plant juices to dye their hair. I thought the red might look nice in yours. What do you think? If you don't like it, I can ask about some other options."

"No," I murmured, mostly just in awe that she'd gone through the trouble of finding all of this for me. "It's great."

I could feel Mycel's grin on the side of my face as I continued to look down into the basket. "A few more options for makeup, though…" she told me, pulling some smaller jars, vials, and pouches from the basket. "Charcoal, arrowroot, spirulina, aloe vera, almond oil… apparently when you mix the right ingredients together, you get some iteration of foundation, mascara, eye shadow… we'll have to get creative." She held another jar up to the light, and we both watched as the tan viscous oil slid down the side of the glass. "I promise, once all of this is over, we'll go back to Sephora." When she looked over at me, we both burst into laughter.

"This is adventurous, even for you," I told her, unable to stifle a snort. I didn't mind being adventurous; in fact, I kind of liked the idea of being a scientist and concocting little potions with my best friend.

"It's a good thing you're already stunning and this is just for fun, then." Mycel chuckled to herself as she pulled the last items from the basket and held them up in front of me. First was a floor-length blue dress made of a heavy fabric that felt a lot like velvet. But when she pulled out the fur shawl that accompanied it, I must've been staring in shock. "It'll keep you warm." When I didn't answer, Mycel raised an eyebrow. "What? Not your style?"

"No, I'm just… shocked that someone who's, like, queen of the forest would have a garment made of… is that cougar fur?"

Mycel laughed again, then gave me an understanding nod. She rubbed the fur between her fingers, and her expression went solemn. "It's not a textile we have a lot of… and I'm sure whoever created it made use of the rest of the animal. I don't know what happened to this cougar, but its death wasn't in vain. Clove says this shawl has been shared among our people for many decades." When she looked at me again, she offered a soft smile and set the shawl down so gently it almost seemed like she was handling a still-living creature. "Now, let's figure out how to turn all of this," she said, gesturing to the vials and jars once again, "into makeup. Maybe you can work your magick to help me with these bags under my eyes."

CHAPTER SEVEN

EARWYN

e were wed in a bright, cold clearing in the forest near the spot where Mycel had been crowned. The air was so crisp that it stung my nose; even if I got my magick back, I imagined the coldness of the winter forest would still chill me to the bone. It wasn't like the frozen depths of the ocean. To me, the ocean felt vast and vulnerable, an open space with nowhere to hide, whereas the layers of foliage and small ecosystems within the forest felt like a safe, nestled home even in the cold. While the purpose of our renewed vows was clear to everyone, it was hard for me to focus on. All I could think of was my wife. I was obsessed. Perhaps even more so given what we had been through together since our last ceremony. This woman had gone to hell and back for me; she'd gone to my literal, personal hell to pull me out. She'd traveled across the continent to acquire allies while I sat by, powerless. She'd soothed me, held me through the loss of my best friend, through Zara's loss, too. To top it all off, she had sacrificed her body to grow our son; she'd taken some tiny contribution from me and turned it into a living, breathing being.

All this, on top of leading a campaign to save her people and others from the brutality of mine. And for what? Love. It was that simple. She did all that she did out of love for her people, her family, her friends, and the earth.

What if she hadn't? What if she had just been herself, in her most basic form – a laughing, spritelike goddess with fiery hair and a big attitude – and existed by my side? As I waited for her at the altar, I thought, what if she had just been Mycel, without any of the extra sacrifice? Well, that would've been more than enough and more than I deserved. She was stunning and admirable without any sacrifice, but the presence of it made her even more unbelievable. I wanted nothing more than to give her back what she'd given me, and so I prayed silently for the return of my magick, so that I could destroy swaths of Ulmosi with my power, so that I could use my body for good. Finally, for once. I wanted, needed, to be her weapon in this war. In fact, the thought gave me a thrill.

"Hey, Romeo," Zara whispered harshly as I stood at the end of the forest's makeshift aisle. She stood on the opposite side of the altar awaiting her best friend, her hair freshly recut into a mohawk and dyed with pops of red; Mycel had scrounged together some materials from her people to make hair dye and makeup for Zara that morning after learning how much she missed some components of the human world. "Your girl is coming."

I didn't know who Romeo was, but I smiled as I caught sight of "my girl." At the end of the aisle, Mycel appeared in her cream-colored dress from the night before. Maz flew behind her, pulling up the trailing end of the dress off the forest floor. She was barefoot. It made my heart flutter. All around us, Mycel's people sat and stood in silence, in awe of their queen. Clove sat near the front of the crowd on a fallen tree, holding a cooing Evren Firth on her lap. Genny was stationed at her feet, her presence giving me the boost of confidence I needed; would I ever not be intimidated by the fact that Mycel was my wife? In the sea of faces, which had become a blur since Mycel's arrival, I also noticed Reed near the back. He stood with his arms across his chest, his expression stern and silent. Before my welcomed distraction, I'd been curious about his thoughts, his intent. Though he was mentally recording this event for their people's archives, I couldn't help but wonder what else was going on behind his gaze. Did the historian add his own commentary to the memories he collected? Did his opinion color the events recorded? Perhaps he'd delete this altogether if it bothered him enough...

I allowed myself to focus on Mycel as she approached the altar, and when her hand slipped into mine so that I could bring her up to join me, it felt so much like the first time we'd made contact. Back then, Mycel had been the less graceful, the less steady of the two of us, and I had helped her awkwardly stumble her way up the stairs to her apartment, where she'd kissed me. I'd never forget that moment, but we were both so different now from the people we had been then. I pressed a kiss into the back of her hand, breathing a sigh of relief when we were standing across from each other, face-to-face. There was something so comforting about her gaze; it felt like home. Maz landed nearby, observing quietly, but no doubt keeping Mycel entertained with a witty quip based on what I knew about their relationship.

In a perfect world, perhaps one of Mycel's aunts would have offici-ated our wedding, had one not been locked away for treason. Perhaps more of my friends would have been present... Well, just one in partic-ular. But despite all that, it was as perfect a second wedding as one could hope. One of the Yannavi elders, Betulia, presided over our union. She was tiny, barely over half my height, and had wrinkles the configuration of which I'd never seen on another being. All of her appeared to sag, like the branches of a willow tree, and moss hung from her drooping earlobes. Even so, her spirit was undoubtedly bright and cheerful, just unhurried. Betulia's words were gentle, kind, the spirit of the forest obvious in them. Our vows were more simplistic this time, partially because we weren't afforded weeks to work on them but also because the depth and passion of our initial vows felt too personal to share with so many. Still, they captured the essence of our bond.

"We are gathered here today, in the beauty of our home, to witness and celebrate the marriage of Mycel and Earwyn. We come together not to mark the start of a relationship, but to acknowledge and strengthen a bond that already exists," Betulia began, speaking with the ease and wisdom of someone who had officiated many weddings over her lengthy life. "A wedding is a celebration of the magick between two people in love, and that's why we are here today – to share in that magick and to reunite Earwyn with his by welcoming him into the Yannavi with open arms. May the life you choose to share abundantly fulfill each of you, inspiring you to give generously to your people and the world. May the promises you make here today reflect the love and sincerity of your truest intention for this union. When life is peaceful and when it is painful, may you continuously be reminded of the beauty and deepest commitment of the vows you make here." She looked to our audience with a smile.

"May you be fulfilled by each other's love and friendship. May you be overjoyed by the promises you are about to make and the life you are creating together. Remember that in every marriage, there are struggles and victories, times of bounty and times of hardship. Marriage is one of life's greatest adventures, enhanced by the love, trust, and dedication you share in one another. May the promises you make to one another today be lived out to the end of your days." Betulia looked to Mycel first, addressing her by her name, then to me. "Mycel and Earwyn, do you, with your people as witnesses, present yourselves willingly and wholeheartedly to be joined in marriage?"

We responded in unison: "We do."

I cleared my throat, the idea of professing my love for Mycel in front of the Yannavi a bit daunting. "Mycel," I said, taking her hands in mine and looking into her eyes. I allowed myself to simply enjoy her gaze for a moment and found that I was calmed, refocused, when I spoke again. "I vow to love and cherish you… to weather every storm with you… to scale any mountain we encounter… and to faithfully love you forever, with all of my heart."

Mycel's gaze glittered with unshed tears. "Earwyn," she responded, giving my hands a soft squeeze. "I vow to love and cherish you… to nurture your soul and watch it bloom… to come back to you, like the ocean does the shore, no matter how far our adventures take us… and to faithfully love you forever, with all of my heart."

Betulia gave us a nod of support before resuming her speech. "Mycel and Earwyn, may your life together be immersed in love and excitement. May you strive to enrich each other in every possible way. And may you work to spread the peace that you share to our people and the rest of the world." She raised her head to address the crowd again and said, "Having pledged their fidelity to one another, to love, honor, and cherish one another in the presence of this gathering and by the power vested in me by Mother Nature, it is my honor to now pronounce you husband and wife and to welcome Earwyn as the new king of Yannava."

And then, in an act that I'd experienced many times before but would never tire of, Mycel kissed me. I was plunged into the depths of her warmth, like being consumed by fire in the midst of this frigid winter landscape. Heat bloomed in my chest and stretched through my body… its tendrils like roots, like flowing magma. My fingers tingled. My heart pounded. I felt like I might burst from the excitement of it all, the novelty, despite having done it so many times before.

Much like Mycel's own crowning ceremony, the trees then reached out to welcome me with a gnarled and intricate crown of branches and vines, more jagged than my wife's but no less beautiful. The snap of the crown separating itself from the tree that had grown it echoed through our surroundings. The frigid wood sent a chill down my spine as it nestled into my hair against my scalp. I reached up to touch it, tracing the pointed outline, admiring each angular detail, and wondered what made it so different from Mycel's. Perhaps the forest was not used to creating a crown for a king, given that Yannava had a history of being ruled by women, or perhaps it was a visual representation of my flawed nature, whereas Mycel, even in all of her struggles, was a soft and elegant being. The connection of the crown and my body sent a wave of electricity through me, though it was hard to tell if that was my magick returning or simply the excitement of the wedding and being welcomed so openly into a new community. Not once had I received this level of warmth from my own people, and the crown I wore in Ulmos felt more like a helmet meant to keep me anchored, weighed down. This one was light, freeing, though I didn't dare take the responsibility that came with it lightly.

The Yannavi – *our people* – cheered.

Rhodes whooped loudly in true Rhodes fashion, and I could've sworn I saw the shimmer of a tear in his eyes, but I wouldn't dare bring it up to him. Ever. Thatcher let out yells of excitement that sounded much like his animal counterpart; the near-growl reverberated through my body. Maz squawked in celebration, and Evren Firth squealed as if he had an idea of what was going on. Perhaps he was just excited by everyone else's excitement, or maybe he had more intuition than we gave him credit for.

Mycel hugged her best friend.

And shortly after, the clearing was nearly empty once again. Betulia shuffled away from the altar with a speed that surprised me, and Elan found us in the shifting crowd, coming over to congratulate us and give both of us hugs that lasted so long I thought she might never let go. It was nice. People returned to their pre-war tasks, and Clove, who was growing as close to Evren as we were, took him to the treehouse for a nap. Celebration was important, yes, but we had no idea when and if my magick would return. There were too many pressing matters at hand for the entire village to wait around and see. I, for one, was grateful that I wouldn't be under the added pressure of observation. When we were alone again, I couldn't help but kiss my wife.

CHAPTER EIGHT

MYCEL

When he pulled away from our kiss, the blue depths of Earwyn's irises crashed like swirling waves. Dangerous. Lethal, even.

CHAPTER NINE

EARWYN

Regaining my magick felt like being plunged into the sea. My surroundings were a blur, and even Mycel faded away from view momentarily. Then, everything was magnified. There was no gust of winter air, but the chime of the breeze caressing each individual leaf and strand of fur in the forest. The rush of the nearby river was amplified. I could feel the frigid, winding strands of water intermingling with each other and each worn river rock as they moved; those sensations were so bold that they may as well have been coming from within my own veins. They whispered a tale of the coming spring and how they longed for the sun to heat their surface. When I returned to my body, I gasped. My muscles were on fire, as if I'd just put them through strenuous activity, and they were full, swollen like I'd lifted boulder after boulder. I felt strong… stronger than I had before, even with my magick. I looked to Mycel again, whose fair face was streaked with concern, and found that every golden flake in her forest-green gaze glimmered brilliantly, like a thousand illuminated stars.

Before I could spend more time admiring her, movement stirred in the corner of my vision and caught my attention. "Wait."

I was already down the aisle when Mycel called after me, her voice laced with confusion and concern. "Wait, no, what do you mean, 'wait'? Where are you going? What is it, Wyn?"

I was on Reed in an instant; the longing glance he'd given Mycel as he dawdled leaving the wedding had not escaped me, but I didn't think he'd meant it to. It was a threat. *He* was a threat. We hit the ground hard, the two of us not small by any means, and I had my hands around his thick neck before he seemed to grasp what had hit him. I was trembling with fury, and the forest spun around me.

Mycel was yelling, but all I could make out was the faint impression of her panicked voice.

"What's your problem?" Reed said through gritted teeth, gripping my wrists. His fingers dug into my flesh as he attempted to pull me off of him and failed. He was strong, but I was stronger. I didn't know how long this would last or if it was just a side effect of me regaining strength after so long without it, but I was determined to take advantage. Not only that, but I was angry… angrier than I'd ever been, and all of that rage needed somewhere to go, someone to go to. Reed felt like the perfect target.

"You." My voice was husky, raw.

"You really want to kill me in front of Mycel?" His gaze flicked over my shoulder. It was then that I realized that my wife was pulling on me as hard as she could, attempting to free Reed from my grasp. I had hardly registered her touch before that moment. Her voice was still muffled under the pounding of my blood in my ears.

"Earwyn, let him go! You're not thinking straight!"

The other man took advantage of my moment of distraction and shoved me off of him, sending me flying onto my back. The ground trembled with impact. My crown, so new to me that it had barely left an impression in my hair, went tumbling off into the woods surrounding the clearing.

Carefully dodging our mutual love interest, I pursued Reed again, rage boiling within me. Despite the cold of the forest, I was on fire. I caught him by his leg as he scrambled away and pulled him toward me. "In front of her, out of her sight, I don't care… yes, I want to kill you!" My voice was raspy, deep and guttural, so different from my usual tone that it took a moment for me to register that I was speaking and not some alternate personality living within my body. Seconds later the sharp crack of splintering bone reverberated through my fist as it collided with the other man's face. I knew he would heal quickly, and that just made me angrier; I wanted him to suffer. He fought back just as hard, and though I was completely consumed by regaining my advantage over him, I was frequently aware of just how close we were to Mycel. If she got hurt during this, then there would be even more hell to pay.

Reed landed several blows himself, initially acting out of self-defense, but eventually succumbing to his own apparent anger.

When I caught one of his fists and gripped his fingers hard between mine, I stared him in the eyes. "I've seen the way you look at her," I told him with a snarl.

"Congratulations," Reed hissed. "You want an award for having eyes?"

"Tell me, do you replay memories of Mycel whenever you miss her?"

The other man finally looked insulted. "That's none of your business."

"Like hell it's not," I growled, gripping his hand so tightly that several fingers crunched. The sticky wetness of blood trickled between our joined hands, and the tang of iron filled the air. "She's not yours to fantasize about anymore!"

Reed bit back a howl of pain and winced, struggling to maintain eye contact with me. His eyes watered, but he didn't relent. I hated that about him, hated that his persistence was showing itself in more ways than one. "She's supposed to be!"

"Let him go!" The other man's retort had me tempted to drag him to the river and drown him. Or perhaps I'd just summon enough water to drown him on dry land and watch him succumb to the power he'd likely been doubting since my arrival. But when Mycel placed a desperate hand on my shoulder once more and spoke, I froze. "Earwyn, stop! He's not the enemy here!"

"Mycel."

My wife's voice was suddenly calm and firm, her breath slowing when she realized that I was capable of listening to her again. "Save it for the people who really deserve it, Wyn."

Even though it felt a lot like Reed deserved every ounce of fire I had within me, I relented. My grip loosened on the other man's fingers in an instant, and I dropped them. They immediately began snapping and crunching, each digit gradually returning to its original place and his skin beginning the mending process already. The forest returned to view, slowly, as my breathing stilled, but when I looked down at Reed, who had stumbled backward and was gripping his injured hand, I still felt the same hatred I'd felt for him earlier. "You should learn your place," I spat.

"Reed, get out of here," Mycel said firmly as she took her place by my side.

Reed's eyes widened in disbelief, and he rubbed his hand, which was almost completely back to normal, as he looked up at my wife. "Mycel, are you kidding m—"

"Don't say her fucking name," I snipped, ready to lunge at him again.

Mycel chimed in again, her hand still on my arm as if she could hold me back, and warned Reed. "Go."

Silence filled the air once we were alone again and I couldn't bring myself to look my wife in the eyes. Mycel's gaze was on me, though, and it felt like my flesh would melt from that focused attention alone. When she sighed, I was filled with shame. Not regret, just shame. "That was not what I expected to be your first act as king."

I finally met her gaze, expecting to find humor in her expression, but there wasn't. "You didn't see the way he was looking at you, Mycel," I explained. "I can feel it, when he's around; he's fantasizing about you. He shouldn't be able to leverage his position in your community to replay his memories of you. They're not his to have anymore."

She shook her head. "How do you know he does that?"

I looked away and sucked my teeth, trying not to seem snarky in my response. "I may be a patient, mostly gentle man, Mycel, but I'm still a man. You think he looks at you with anything but lust, longing? Doubtful. I don't want to imagine how he uses those vivid memories when I can't even hear your name or smell your perfume without getting hard. It's not like he was looking at Zara…"

My wife was silent as she processed my commentary, and I braced for whatever the backlash of beating her ex-lover would be. I decided then that it would be worth it. I hadn't even fatally harmed him, but if beating the shit out of him left me in trouble with my partner, then I'd deal with the consequences gladly. When we locked eyes once more, I set my jaw. "Go on then, lay into me." We'd never had that type of relationship that humans complained about, the one where the wife was the nag to a human who felt hellishly bound to her, but I braced for reprimand anyway.

What I didn't expect, however, was the force of her crushing her lips to mine to send me stumbling backward. I caught both of us, my arms reflexively shooting out to wrap around her and steady us, then hesitantly returned the advance. Before I knew it, we were exploring each other's mouths with an eagerness I hadn't seen from my wife in a while, and she hitched her leg around my waist as if to climb me. My cock was hard in an instant, just like I'd told her, and the influx of sensation distracted me from my confusion. I growled against the plush warmth of my wife's lips and backed her against a nearby tree, where my fingers quickly found the hem of her dress and shoved it up to her hips. I wanted her. I needed her. I wanted to fuck every memory of Reed from her body. But when I gripped her thigh roughly enough to elicit a whimper, I forced myself to pause. "Mycel… Mycel, you need to stop."

"Why? What's wrong?" She removed her hands from me quickly, like she always did when I indicated I might be uncomfortable, and I wished she would've lingered just a little longer. It meant so much to me that she always erred on the side of caution, though.

I searched Mycel's gaze as I struggled to find the words to explain myself; in true male form, it was difficult for me to think straight in moments like this. "It's not for me, it's for you. It's a lot… the influx of sensation from getting my magick back. If you keep kissing me, I'm not sure I'll be able to control myself."

Mycel looked at me curiously, and I detected a hint of disappointment on her face.

"Besides, Evren is still so little and…" I wasn't sure how to phrase my concerns.

"It's okay. I'm healed."

My eyes widened. Clearly, I knew nothing about childbirth. Or magick as it related to childbirth. Was it like that for humans, too? Hell, why did I care? "Oh. Well… believe me, it's not that I don't want to."

"Then do it," she said plainly, challenging me in a way that was very unlike her. The confidence in her expression was unmistakable; she was egging me on.

I bit my lip, unsure of how to respond. "Do what?"

"Take me," she shrugged. "I'm yours, aren't I?"

I reached up to run my thumb across her lower lip, which was already red and swollen from our passionate kissing. Her breath was hot on my flesh and smelled like berries. "Yes. But are you ready for me?" I was thick and hard, and my body felt like a rippling mass of destruction.

Mycel nipped at my finger, then grabbed my hand to return it to her thigh. She guided me beneath the fabric of her dress, to the edge of her panties, where she invited my eager fingers in. I brushed the slit of her pussy and found her damp, drenched... and all for me. What a gift. "To what do I owe this pleasure?"

"I'm wet from watching you fight, Wyn."

I would've almost forgotten about the prior altercation if not for the slight soreness already brewing in my body and the blood on my brow from a particularly lucky shot that Reed had snuck in. I grunted in response to her comment and yanked her panties down her thighs, not wanting to waste a moment. When I was too impatient to get them all the way off, a swift tug tore one hip of the garment and gave me full access to her. I needed her desperately and immediately, so I unbuckled my belt with one hand while her own roamed over my chest and arms, squeezing and exploring as they moved. "You like it when I lose control," I told her, my voice low and unrecognizable again. Who the hell was I? I hoisted her legs up onto my waist so that she was straddling me, her warm, inviting cleft only inches from the part of me that was straining for her.

"I do," she purred.

"Enough to come on my cock over and over?"

"If you make me," Mycel quipped. Her lips were parted to say more, but she was immediately silenced when I gripped myself and slid into her deftly. My head fell back against my will, and the sound that left my throat must've been akin to a wild animal because the forest clearing was suddenly void of all creature noise. Not a single bird shuffled in the trees.

"I'd love nothing more." My wife's eyes fluttered shut, and when I focused on her face again, I couldn't help but tsk at her. "Eyes on me. Look at me when I make you come. Look at your king." Mycel looked at me once more, and her body tightened in response, her pussy gripping me reflexively at my commentary. "Good."

The rest of our interaction was quieter, with less banter and more eagerness in each whine and sigh. I was certain that I was leaving marks on my wife's skin: on her hips and thighs, on the sides of her neck when I pulled her close for a frantic kiss as I hammered into her. I brought her to the edge of her cliff of pleasure time and time again, only letting her fall over occasionally while I held her close, and each frantic, divine cry of her climax brought me closer to mine. I was drenched in sweat, despite the climate around us, and felt nowhere near fatigued, despite how long we'd been there, despite holding my wife up with my arms alone. The feeling of her juices dripping down my balls spurred me on. What a compliment, I thought, but as my own orgasm raced nearer, I crushed my lips to hers again before meeting her gaze. "One more, stay with me."

"Yes," she breathed. As her grip on my arms began to slip, she dug her nails into my flesh and threw one arm around my neck, causing it to brush against my tender, newly opened gills. I let out a hiss in response. "Sorr—"

"More," I grunted, still thrusting into her at an even pace. I moved her hand onto my shoulder and pressed it into me hard, willing her to grip me there. Sore gills were one thing, but I ached from the half-moon marks of my wife's nails in my flesh.

Mycel's eyes widened in response, but she must've gotten the message from my expression because she gripped me harder. When she bent her head toward my chest to bite into my pec, I crumbled immediately. "Hell, goddess… that's it," I grunted, thrusting harder just as I spilled myself into her. "Squeeze me, Mycel, milk the come out of me. Show me how badly you want it." I hammered into her until I had nothing left to give, and she followed shortly after, coming around my now-sensitive prick as she bit rough kisses into the side of my neck.

Eventually the demands on my body caught up with me, and I lowered us to the ground in exhaustion, but my cock was ready to go again only moments later. I forced myself to lie down and rest, if only for a moment, and Mycel snuggled against my chest. Our clothes were scattered on the ground around us, and I remembered that somewhere out there, on the forest floor, there was a crown that supposedly belonged to me. I'd have to find it later.

Mycel traced her slender fingers across the flesh of my chest and warned me, "Don't kill any of our people, okay?"

"Fine, but only because you asked," I told her with a sigh. "I can't guarantee I won't beat the shit out of one in particular if he doesn't stand down, though." The rest of them were probably safe with me, but Reed and Hyssop were ones to keep an eye on.

Before Mycel could quip a response, she was pulling herself upright as if she'd heard something far off in the woods. "Is that you?"

My ears twitched, and if I were an animal, they would've turned toward the sounds of the forest. Still, I couldn't place what she was referring to. "What do you mean?"

"The water is rising again," she said, her voice laced with concern. Could she hear each trickle, each individual droplet of water as I had earlier?

"No, it's not me. I haven't really tried much since my magick returned." Except for trying to kill your ex-lover. Otherwise, no, not much.

"Then they're trying to scare us, to get us to leave," she mused, reaching for her dress which lay in a tattered pile nearby. "Maybe they think we'll surrender and avoid the fight altogether." I watched Mycel from my spot on the ground as she tuned into the forest, no doubt gathering more information than I could. Perhaps one day I'd be as in-tune with the home of the Yannavi as she was. Soon, she'd pulled her dress over her body, but not before I could appreciate the new details that I hadn't noticed in the frenzy of our lovemaking. Motherhood and the journeys she'd been on while pregnant had changed her body. While she'd healed quickly following childbirth, signs of our child remained; her belly looked softer, with stretch marks that resembled pinkish lightning bolts. Her breasts were bigger, fuller, and they bounced as she adjusted her dress. All of her travel and training had made her arms stronger, too, and more defined. Mycel had always been the essence of beauty to me, but there was something deep and delicious about watching her change with life's experiences. I wanted to worship her.

"Well, that's not going to happen." We needed to gather our people. I had just buttoned up my pants when the sound of small paws scampering through the woods caught my attention. There were a lot of paws in the forest, but these were familiar… a set I hadn't been in tune with enough to actually hear for a long time. Seconds later, Genny bounded into the clearing and sought me out, meeting my gaze with an intensity that hadn't been there since we lost our connection. She flopped down in front of me and tilted her head to the side. "Hey, girl…"

"What is it?" Mycel asked when she noticed that I'd stopped dressing.

"I can hear her," I said quietly before sitting on the ground in front of my familiar. I wiped my face with the back of my hand before the little otter leapt into my lap, rolling onto her back over and over in excitement as small chirps and clicks emanated from her. That's what they sounded like on the outside, at least, but between the two of us, she was exclaiming her excitement over our reunion. I'd never heard her so ecstatic before.

It's you, it's you, oh I've missed you so much! Don't you ever do that again! It was so quiet, Earwyn, I was so lost! I was so worried!

I rubbed behind her ears, almost unable to get my fingers into her fur with the way she continued to tumble in my lap. "I know, I know," I told her with a laugh. "I missed you, too!"

* * *

THERE WASN'T MUCH TIME TO WASTE, EVEN WITH THE LINGERING excitement of the wedding in the air. We couldn't wait until the next morning to address everyone. I cleared my throat and surveyed the group of Yannavi, my new people, who had joined us outside of our treehouse upon our return. It was intimidating. I reminded myself that this was not the same group of people who had watched me deteriorate on my throne or be knocked down on a regular basis by my bride-to-be. Back then, I'd done very little in the way of actually commanding or ruling my people; on paper, I was their leader, but in person, I was nothing but a placeholder, someone to warm the throne until Maren was able to take her rightful place in charge, produce an heir that she could puppeteer and groom, and probably have me killed in my sleep. Who was I kidding? Being killed in my sleep suggested that Maren cared about my comfort... no, she probably would have made the suffering last. She seemed to like that. I was spiraling in thought as I faced my new people, people who, if they were anything like Mycel, would accept me and fight by my side.

I swallowed hard, willing my lips and tongue, desiccated from anxious panting, to wet themselves so that I could speak. Where was the confidence I'd had when facing Reed in the clearing? That certainly would've been helpful. This was new, I reminded myself... I had a clean slate, and the hearts of the Yannavi were much bigger and more forgiving than those of the Ulmosi. I opened my mouth as if to speak, but stammered, unable to find the right words. Then, Rhodes jabbed me in the back harder than necessary. "Go on then."

"You got this," whispered Zahir from somewhere behind me.

Eyes of green and gold stared out at me from the group, like sunlight and foliage working together in perfect harmony. They looked so much like Mycel's. Did they look at my endless blue gaze and see the enemy?

Again, I cleared my throat and prayed for the Earwyn who'd given impassioned charity ball speeches about the ocean to come through in my delivery; he acted like he knew what he was talking about, but I hadn't seen that man in a very long time. That Earwyn had been buttoned up in fancy suits, wound tight by the need to impress people, and so rigid that it was a wonder he didn't shatter into a million pieces upon meeting Mycel's free spirit. "First things first; you all need to learn to swim. Being able to fight is useless if you're unable to survive the water. That's going to be their first weapon. Those who are too young or unwell to swim will be kept high up in guarded tree-houses, but the rest of you need to be able to stay afloat in the water so that you can climb back up to the trees if needed. Children, too," I added, looking at the young ones in our group.

"How young?" a woman who appeared maybe twenty in human years piped up. She had a toddler on her hip who was absentmind-edly sucking on a lock of her mother's hair; it was balled up in her tiny fist. I imagined Evren doing the same to Mycel or myself one day and my heart ached.

"She's probably too young," I told her, unsure of exactly how old the child was but comparing her to my memory of the children in Ulmos as well as I could.

The mother's brow furrowed, and she loosened the baby's grip from her hair before asking, "Don't Ulmosi babies learn how to swim early?"

"Sure, but it's in their blood. I'd rather we keep the small ones out of harm's way than try to keep track of them in the water. If we have time, we can try to teach them… but it's going to take longer than for most of the adults."

The woman eyed me curiously for a moment, as if still determining if she could trust me, then nodded. I stifled a sigh of relief; at least she believed me enough to temporarily cease her questioning.

"We'll have our friends, the Alaskans, with us," I continued, returning to the entire group. "They can freeze sheets of water into ice for you to climb onto if needed, but there are only a few of them, so we can't rely on them to rescue everyone who falls in. We're grateful for their help and need to protect them as our own." My phrasing felt foreign. In my heart, I believed that I was one of them, but I wouldn't have been surprised if they didn't believe we were a united group yet. I had a lot to prove. Mycel did, too, but her bravery and commitment had shown in her return to Yannava and her vulnerability in sharing her memories.

From behind me, Thatcher gave a soft grunt of approval. Had he wondered if this battle would result in the loss of any of his rather large family? The thought had kept me up at night. When they arrived, the timeline of which was yet to be determined, they'd be leaving their human counterparts back in Utqiagvik. Did they all understand the inherent risk of entering into this war with us? They'd told us it was worth it to them to protect the humans that they'd grown so close to, but would they still feel that way if they returned to Alaska as a smaller family?

"That'd be much appreciated." A voice had sounded from the back of the group. Though I hadn't met them yet, I could guess who had just arrived based on Thatcher's reaction alone. A grin spread across his face before he had even turned to face his parents, and when he did, he immediately ran to them and nearly tackled the pair. His father let out a hearty laugh, and I suddenly felt a little lighter, too. "We intend to emerge victorious," Owen stated as he ruffled his son's hair. "What can we do to help prepare?"

I realized it was my turn to put the plan into action. "Let's split up. The bears..." I gave Owen, Nora, and Thatcher a look to see if they minded being referred to that way, even though I knew that Nora's varispirit form was actually a fox. When they didn't protest, I continued. "…Zahir, and I will take different groups to parts of the river for lessons. Maybe Rhodes…" I thought aloud, then glanced over at my best friend's twin.

"Maybe Rhodes *what*?"

"You can teach people to swim."

I should've known better than to suggest it because he practically started laughing in my face.

"You ever seen a shark in a river?"

I tried to remain neutral and avoid rolling my eyes. "In your *human* form." *Dumbass.* Before he could argue more, I continued to the group, "There should be some deeper sections. If not…" I looked over my shoulder at Reed. "We'll need to create a makeshift pool that's deep enough for swimming."

Reed nodded, flexing his hands. I had no doubt he could unearth a tremendous tree or simply dig enough of a hole to create a swimming spot for practice. I could fill it. I hoped that our earlier altercation would keep him in his place and he'd focus on helping the group rather than picking another fight with me. Since my immense burst of strength I felt earlier hadn't started to fade yet, I felt confident that I still had the upper hand.

"Zahir, we'll need fires for people to warm themselves once they're out of the water. It's going to be cold, they're not used to being soaking wet in the middle of winter… and we'll be practicing every day until the Ulmosi arrive." It was no longer an "if" but a "when." I didn't wait for Zahir's response, because I knew he would agree to do whatever was needed.

I looked up to the balcony of the treehouse I shared with Mycel, who had been silently observing my speech with a smile on her face and Maz on her shoulder, then back to the group of people. "Those of you who aren't actively in swimming lessons with us today, please join our queen in the armory if you're old enough to fight. You should be fitted for armor and a weapon that works for your body and level of strength; she can help you with that." I nodded firmly, trying to assure myself that I could be confident in what I had said. Meanwhile, my cock twitched at the mention of "our queen." If an increased libido was part of regaining my magick, I surely hoped that war would have enough breaks to sate it. "If you're unable to join her, Reed will meet you there after we're done at the river."

Reed's voice was thick with irritation. "I will?"

"You will," I said sternly under my breath.

He bristled behind me, but we didn't have time to discuss it further, nor did I want to make it a commonplace thing that we'd discuss all of my decisions. What part of learning his place did he not understand? Now that his hand was healed, it seemed he didn't feel very inclined to stand down. I didn't know much about Yannavi rule, but my assumption was that being king and married to the ruling queen gave me some sort of say in how things were run. It was time for action. If the Ulmosi arrived the next day, these people would not be prepared; they would live out another one of Mycel's nightmares and perish in the water as they had before. I'd seen my fair share of people drown at the hands of Ulmosi rule and would not let that happen again under my watch. They could learn to swim; water was part of the forest, too, and was not a foreign element to them. Perhaps some already had a basic understanding of how to navigate deep water. Mycel did, after all. Before breaking off into groups, I added, "If you will not be fighting, we need you to gather provisions and begin stocking all of the treehouses with enough materials to last a while. Blankets, in case they come soon while it's cold or someone falls into the water… food, water, provisions… Although I hope this will be over quickly, the last thing we need is for people to go hungry while waiting for the storm to pass."

Someone piped up suddenly from the group. "And what if they take down the trees?"

Before I could respond, Mycel spoke. Perhaps she sensed some sort of doubt from the group that I couldn't quite gauge; despite her time away, she would always know her people better than I did. "Then we need to create a way to get from one tree to another," she told them, leaning on the rail of the treehouse more casually than I'd ever seen a ruler do. She looked so approachable, but almost like a means to luring prey in. "Bridges, pulleys, anything that will help us transport people across quickly... and make sure that the provisions in each treehouse are kept in easy-to-move packages; if we have to go from one tree to another, we won't have time to pack. Parents, make sure your children know when to move... and those with young babies, let's ensure each family has a wrap to transport them quickly. They may take down the weaker trees, but we know that so many of these would be impossible for them to sway."

I nodded up at her in agreement and gratefulness for her quick thinking. She winked at me. My heart may have stopped. Before I could respond, she added, "I doubt our archers will let them get that far, however."

"Well, I'll be damned," Reed muttered. "She sure thought that up quick." I wouldn't have been surprised if he had shot her a playful glance. Well, maybe. The old Reed would have without a doubt used this as an opportunity to flirt with her, but he had been acting strange lately... maybe even distracted by something other than Mycel. Thankfully, it was the least of my concerns.

My audience immediately began talking amongst themselves, but thankfully Zahir, with all of the energy in the world, piped up. "I'll take one group!" he said clearly above the chatter. When it died down, he drew a line in the air between the group of people, splitting off a smaller section for him to take the lead of. "From you... to you, let's go. Can someone lead me to the closest body of water? Neeri, come along, you can help teach some of the kids." His daughter followed closely behind with a spring in her step. Both of them were bundled up in layers of clothing from the Alaskans, no doubt having never experienced extended cold like in the forest. I didn't envy how they'd react to the bitter cold of the stream, but it was nice to know that despite the frigid cold, despite the impending war, children could still find something to look forward to. Neeri would have new friends, and that was enough for her. Meanwhile, I couldn't imagine the fear going through Zahir's mind. I made a mental note to discuss our plan for Neeri with both Zahir and Mycel… as scrappy and capable as she was, she was too young to fight, and I would never be able to live with myself if she got hurt, let alone killed. Perhaps she could stay with Evren Firth.

Soon, I followed Zahir's lead and had my own group following me. Thatcher took the last bunch, and I sent Reed along with him for a break from his side commentary. My group moved parallel to Zahir's, and as we walked through the woods, the frosted ground crunching sharply under our steps, Zahir shot me a sideways glance through his wild tangle of black hair. He smiled, and in his gaze, I saw a flash of Anala. "How's fatherhood treating you?"

It was such a normal, casual, and kindhearted thing to ask… something you might ask a good friend over coffee on any day of the week. Hadn't I asked that question when I worked with humans? I allowed myself a second to smile and feel hopeful that he might ask again one day, in a different setting. "Good."

A few more steps in silence and Zahir grasped at another attempt to connect. "You know you gotta… like, feed them multiple times a day, right?"

I chuckled. "Yeah, Neeri taught me that."

"It only took him a couple of days to get the hang of it!" The girl giggled just as we broke off in different directions. The pair brought such lightness to our group that I couldn't help but smile. Neeri. Evren. We'd keep them safe. We had to. I was certain that the Alaskans were bringing joy and smiles to their group as well.

We all parked ourselves and our groups at different points of the stream where it got deepest. Prior to starting our lessons, Zahir and Neeri went through and set up tiny base camps with floating fires for the Yannavi to warm themselves by once they got out of the water. Meanwhile, I knelt at the edge of the water and immersed my hands, closing my eyes and allowing myself to feel my connection to the river. It felt foreign. I hadn't associated myself with this element in so long, and yet… it felt right. I breathed deeply, and the water seemed to match each of my breaths, rising slowly as I willed it to grow with the expanding of my lungs.

When you're born with the ability to swim, teaching others how can be confusing. As I supported villager after villager in learning how to tread water so they could at least stay alive long enough for a strong swimmer to come get them, I fought back the urge to ask them to "just swim!" They weren't averse to water, nor were they new to it, but wading through a shallow pool or stream was much different than being able to tread water for extended periods of time or outswim a predator. I had no doubt that Zahir and Neeri were faring much better than I was, due to their inherently kind and patient nature; my own patience seemed to be on the thin side since my run-in with Reed.

"Like this?" a young Yannavi man with dirty blond hair asked as he floated in front of me.

"Looks great!" I forced enthusiasm just in time to turn and see another person dip under the water as they struggled to paddle. I crooked a finger in their direction and sent a tiny wave to right them again. "Stand up if you need to. It shouldn't be too deep. Then try again." I spoke louder this time so that the whole group could hear me. "If you get tired, practice floating. If you're stuck in the water for too long, you still need to keep yourself alive until someone can pull you out. Don't give up!"

I sighed and wiped water from my face, shoving my hair back away from my eyes where it threatened to freeze in the cold air of winter. "If you're too cold, take a break and warm up, then get back in. Keep moving! Leverage your magick to gather vines or large pieces of bark to float on or pull yourself back into the trees. If swimming is a challenge, we need to get creative." The Yannavi gave me sidelong glances, then a few reassured nods before heading back in the water. Some tapped out earlier than I would have liked, so I encouraged their more confident peers to support them in practicing land magick that could help them. It was only day one, but we also had no idea when our enemies would move in or how. These were my people now, and I needed to protect them.

Sometime later, Owen and Nora joined us; their own group had taken a break, and they wanted to come troubleshoot with the other groups. The purpose of their participation was to help others learn how to swim, but to also practice mounting the Alaskans' backs in bear form so that they could efficiently get people out of the water when and if the time came. So when they arrived in their loud and boisterous manner, talking up everyone in the group and filling the air with rumbling laughter, I was initially displeased. I could just imagine the loss we were at risk for if we didn't take things seriously, and now that I was officially a member of this group and its leadership, I felt even more responsible for every single life that was at stake with the coming confrontation. Optimism was good, cheerfulness we needed, but not at the risk of losing focus.

"Hey, hey, easy on the hair!" Owen growled as he stood in the water, shirtless and being climbed by many shivering young Yannavi children who were still struggling to get used to the temperature of the water. They giggled and scaled the man with ease, almost as if he were a towering cedar. "Oh, come on, you little—" Owen winced as they grabbed fistfuls of graying chest and arm hair to pull themselves up by, then eventually relented and pulled them off of him, plunking each one into the water.

Nearby parents gasped, and when they didn't pop up immediately, Nora waded over in a panic. "They don't know how to swim yet!"

"Ah, come on, it's not that deep! Give 'em a second!" Owen put up a hand toward the adults who were threatening to leap into the stream, though he seemed certain that we'd end up with a whole mess of people needing to be saved if they went forward with that plan. He grumbled a little to himself, and it sounded a lot like *"How're they supposed to learn to swim without trying?"* I couldn't argue with that.

Nora was still a few steps away from her husband when she was pulled down into the water as if her legs had been swept from beneath her, flailing, and she let out a shriek. Seconds later she was floating in the water on her back, cackling loudly as the children who had pulled her under surrounded her in their mock attack.

"Gotcha!" one squealed, splashing the female varispirit. The little boy must've been no older than five and was a soaked, trembling mess, but half of his jitters came from the laughter reverberating through his body. If he and his similarly aged peers could figure it out, perhaps we'd be okay.

"You did, ya little sneak!" Nora exclaimed, hoisting herself upright just in time to chase the child through the water.

Sighs of relief sounded from the observing parents.

"Well, whatdya think, boss?" Owen asked, gesturing at the children milling about in the water. They were doing well. "They can't all be mermaids, but…"

"Not bad," I commended him with a nod and rose from my spot on the bank to gather the attention of the group. "The rest of you… if they can do it, you can as well. The kids might be a bit more fearless, but we're here to help each and every one of you. When we return tomorrow, everyone should be ready to get in the water." I glanced over at a teen girl who had sat cross-armed on the bank nearby during the entire lesson and made a mental note to check in with her if she resumed that position the next day.

As we wrapped up for the evening – the group was exhausted, hungry, and no doubt sick of the water – I was drawn to some commotion further down the stream. Children were both screaming in terror and laughing hysterically, a combination which caused me confusion until I approached the scene. Apparently the Yannavi children hadn't heard of a shark, let alone seen one, so when Rhodes insisted that he could turn into one, they had dared him to "prove it." The result was a giant shark flopping awkwardly in a very shallow pool while the forest folk watched in sheer horror or intense amusement. When I realized that everyone was safe, I rolled my eyes and threw Rhodes's shirt onto the bank so that he wouldn't scar the children with his nudity once he shifted back.

That night in the treehouse I mused aloud to Mycel, who had undoubtedly been busy with her own slew of tasks that day. Because she'd been with Evren Firth for most of the day, toting him with her on her hip or in a wrap, she seemed more at ease than I'd seen her in a while. "I wonder if putting her with Zahir and Thatcher would bring her out of her shell a bit… they're pretty young, too… maybe she's just feeling out of place with all of the kids that were with us today. Or maybe there are other Yannavi her age, and they just ended up in the other groups?" My body was undeniably sore from the day's events, between getting used to my regained magick and having to utilize it for hours on end, but there was something so satisfying about that type of soreness.

Mycel rolled over next to me, having just placed Evren in his crib, and propped herself up on one of her arms while looking at me. Her hair, wavy and wild as ever, tumbled over one of her shoulders. I could smell it from where I lay next to her, the scent floral and heady.

"What is it?"

She smiled. "Nothing, I just haven't seen you this… passionate in a long time."

I couldn't help but chuckle at her phrasing. "You've seen me plenty passionate," I told her, shifting on the bed so that I could pull her into my arms. She settled against my side and rested her head on my chest, where I breathed her in once again.

"You know what I mean," she replied, tracing her fingers down my chest and midsection. Her voice was gentle, honeyed, careful not to wake our son, who had proven to be an awful sleeper. If I dwelled too long on the timing, I'd have thought that the universe was plotting against us; having and raising a child in the midst of a war wasn't ideal, but this one didn't even want his parents to rest. Not only that, but I could see Mycel's anxiousness spike the second he was out of sight, even if it was just with her aunt. I felt bound to him, too, but it was obviously different for her… it was as if her mind could focus on nothing else unless Evren was nearby.

"Yeah…" I stared at the ceiling of the treehouse for a moment, idly tangling a lock of my wife's hair around my fingers. "It feels like I might actually be useful now, like I can bring some value to this fight," I told her. "And finally being on the right side of the fight feels… redemptive."

Mycel shifted against my side again and I could feel her expression change against my chest. Perhaps she was smiling. "I think putting that girl with some others her age is a great idea, Wyn."

That night, I went to sleep feeling the most accomplished I had in a very long time; it finally felt like I was contributing to the fight. That sleep didn't last long, thanks to the restlessness of our infant, but each minute felt well deserved.

CHAPTER TEN

MYCEL

Life felt full of exhausting day after exhausting day. That night, I finally allowed myself to rest, my husband by my side and my son in his crib for the first time rather than in our arms or sandwiched between the two of us.

When the light of morning crept through the thick curtains in our treehouse, however, I woke to an empty crib.

CHAPTER ELEVEN

ZARA

Mycel's scream shook the forest.
Like thunder.
Like an earthquake.
Like the blaring of a thousand car horns at once.
Have you ever been to a Seattle Sounders game? Like that, like the deafening roar of a crowd of thousands chanting, bellowing, stomping.
Like every being on earth should feel her pain.

CHAPTER TWELVE

EARWYN

I woke to Mycel's scream and was certain that every creature within a mile had also been jostled from their sleep, panic stricken into their hearts by the agony in her cry.

Evren Firth was gone.

Our son was gone. Taken. Nabbed from the very crib he was supposed to be safe in, right next to our bed. The previous night had felt too calm, too right, and I should have known something was awry. He was gone.

Everyone was already on high alert for the moment that the Ulmosi army descended on us, but we didn't expect this to be one of their tactics. It took everything in me not to let my mind wander… What would they do with my son? Sure, he could just be a pawn, returned to us upon surrender, but Maren was spiteful, and her cruelty had no bounds; no one was exempt from being harmed by her decision making. My parents were no better. When Mycel's crying ceased suddenly, it was time to act, not panic. I needed to do something. I stumbled out onto the platform of our treehouse to find Reed and a handful of Yannavi soldiers at attention. A few Yannavi had gathered on the ground below, startled by the noise so early in the morning and likely expecting the worst. Silence was a threat.

"Secure the perimeter of the city," I commanded harshly, my voice still raspy and dry from sleep. I knew full well that Mycel could've done the same, but hoped that I could handle things on my own for her. My eyes burned, both from lack of actual rest and the painful reality of trying not to let my emotions get in the way. "No one leaves aside from soldiers. They need to comb every inch of forest for at least five miles in each direction. Whoever took him couldn't have gone far, I just got him back to bed an hour ago."

Reed nodded, not questioning, not commenting. He had come a lot quicker than I'd anticipated, and if not for the chaos we were entrenched in, I would've questioned his motives. Was he afraid of me or just looking for another reason to get in Mycel's good graces again? Perhaps the sound of her heartbreak had struck a chord within him, too. "We'll find him," he bit out. "Tell Mycel we'll find him." I thanked the heavens for his concision. It was a stark difference from the initial reaction that he'd had toward the baby, but I was proud of him for putting his personal feelings aside; Evren Firth needed to be everyone's priority now, just as any other lost child would be in that moment. My stomach turned at the thought of him crying in a stranger's arms; what would they do to silence him? Was he afraid?

Our son had been alive for less than a month and Mycel had already had her share of nightmares about losing him. When the sun was up, and we were both fully awake, she refused to acknowledge them. But in the secrecy of the night, she had cried in my arms while describing the absolute horrors that plagued her; she was no doubt recounting those horrors now as she imagined what Evren's captor was doing with him. Only a few nights prior she had recounted a nightmare that was so vivid, so intense, that I had to shake her from her sleep to stop her hysterical screaming.

"He was sinking!" she said between sobs as I held her in my arms, stroking her sweat-soaked mane.

"He's right there, Mycel, he's next to you. He's not going anywhere."

"I saw him… sinking to the bottom of the ocean… suffocating…" Her chest heaved with each terrible statement, and she trembled uncontrollably. "When I finally got to him, he was blue, Earwyn! I couldn't get him to breathe again! He stopped breathing, he stopped breathing…"

It was only when I pulled Evren from his crib and brought him to his mother so that she could hear his breathing, feel his heartbeat while he nursed, that she calmed a little.

Before I could turn back to the treehouse, Mycel was standing in the doorway, fully equipped. I didn't have time to muse over whether she'd run down to the armory without me noticing or had a personal stockpile of weapons in our dwelling just in case, though she'd confided in me many fears about Evren needing to be protected. She was clad in a thick tunic and pants, her favorite boots, and sheaths and belts that housed a variety of daggers, a sword, and a vial of liquid on her hip that looked deadly without explanation. Her reddened eyes barely wasted a glance on me as she tightened one last strap on her outfit. "Which direction am I going?"

"What are you talking about?" I asked. I needed her to stay put, to stay safe while we figured out where our son had gone… letting her go off into the woods while there was an enemy on the loose just made her another target.

"I'm going to get our son, Wyn." She didn't say it, but I knew that if she wasn't moving, wasn't actively working to find our child, she would feel crazy and out of control. Her gaze was fierce and brimming with rage when she finally looked at me, her use of my nickname the only reason I was certain it wasn't aimed at me. But then again, I had been the one to put him back to bed… How had I not noticed someone entering our home? How had none of us noticed? What about Genny or Maz? As if it mattered anymore… "Which direction needs to be covered? Tell me now, or I'll pick on my own."

Zara had rushed out of the house immediately behind her, trying to pull her back by the edge of her cloak, but was no match strength-wise. She looked as rattled as we all felt and had clearly been roused from sleep by Mycel's screaming, though by the looks of it that sleep had not been particularly restful. She'd headed to our treehouse so soon after our discovery that it almost felt like she'd been ready to act at a moment's notice. That type of loyalty and devotion was not lost on me. "Sprout, come on—"

"We're wasting time." Mycel didn't look at her friend, but addressed the group without holding anyone's gaze. "The longer we argue about this, the further his captor is going to get, and the more danger Evren will be in. We need to intercept his captor before they get back to the water. I don't even know if he'd survive the swim." For a moment, a look of terror replaced the rage in her gaze, and she stared at me with tears welling in her eyes. She had been dragged through the ocean by Rhodes before and knew the pain that came from being unprepared for that type of journey. To imagine our infant son in the same circumstances was horrifying. "We haven't tried, we don't even know if he can swim, and what if he—"

"West," I blurted out finally.

"This has Maren's name all over it!" Mycel yelled as she sped down the treehouse stairs to the forest floor, her feet barely touching the wooden planks as she went. "If I find her, I'll kill her. I'll kill her!" I'd never heard Mycel talk about killing people herself before, but then again, no one had stolen our child before either. I thought about the way that Maren had carelessly sent Anala to her death in the shark bubble and wondered if she'd ever done the same with a child; it would not have surprised me, nor would my parents' apathy about such decisions. How many Ulmosi had lost their children to such a fate, and for what reason? Likely trivial mistakes, not warranting the loss of a life, let alone an innocent child's life, but the Ulmosi rulers were so hardened to the pain they caused…

"I'll go North," I said finally, leaving Zara and Reed behind as I jumped down from the treehouse landing to meet up with the soldiers who would also be going in my direction. The ground trembled, almost as if I'd transferred my own rage directly into the dirt. I couldn't think beyond that except to wonder if this was how Mycel always felt when Evren wasn't in her line of sight. "Zara, Reed, link up," I called to them before taking off with a group of the soldiers. Rhodes was just joining the group when I shouted back at him. "Get the Alaskans and start looking!"

We moved quickly, and I was more grateful for my magick than I thought possible. My brief stint with mortality had shown me the discomfort of a slower travel pace, of increased fatigue, of disconnection with nature. But now… distance flew beneath my steps with ease, the changes in the air told me which direction to go, where to look, and the soldiers of Yannava followed my lead with zero complaint, scouring each foot of land and trees for our shared baby prince. I hoped that the captor was Ulmosi and that their inexperience with the woods would lead to a mistake, but if they had found a way into our bedroom, they likely had an inside scoop… Perhaps it was one of Mycel's people, working directly with Ulmos like Hyssop had been. Or was she still?

Soon the forest was a blur around me, and I realized that I'd covered extensive ground without really thinking. I forced myself to stop, my heart pounding in my ears, and try to listen in for clues. It was hard to focus, knowing that Evren was out there without either of his parents and in the hands of someone who wished him harm. Even if they were just a guard or soldier sent by Ulmos, they were doing evil work for evil people. After Firth, Rhodes, and I all escaped Ulmos, I realized that there was no excuse for others not to turn against them.

The commoners, maybe they had fewer resources and power, but if Rhodes could leave, so could any soldier. They wouldn't be any less safe, and they'd be on the right side of things. How subjective could good and evil actually be when it involved the capture and potential harm of an infant?

As I caught my breath, the sound of the forest returned to my ears instead of just rushing blood, and I closed my eyes.

I tried to really tune in to the forest, which was still new to me, still foreign, despite being my new home.

Again, I felt the breeze through the trees. A rush of water trickling past frozen rocks. And then, there it was, a voice that didn't quite belong in the woods. It was gruff, irritated, somehow familiar, but out of place: *"Shut up, you little bastard."*

My breath hitched in my throat as I waited for the noise in response: Evren's whimpering. I had found them. Judging by the lack of footsteps, they'd stopped, and Evren's captor was attempting to silence him. I wanted to run, to sprint toward the voices, but knew that I could easily be found out and the captor would be on the run once more, possibly putting him completely out of reach. I couldn't risk that. I was gradually making my way through the trees toward the captor's irate muttering when Evren fussed again. My stomach turned.

"If Maren didn't need you alive, you little brat, I'd—"

"You'd what?" I hissed, unable to control myself. I was only a few steps away from them, and the kidnapper's own preoccupation with trying to shush my child had made him oblivious to my approach. When he raised his head to meet my gaze, one of his hands going for the sword at his hip, I reached a hand out toward him on impulse. All around me, the forest spoke to me for the first time; the roots of each towering tree groaned in a way that reverberated within me, and I felt suddenly aligned with every living creature climbing, burrowing, scuttling, scavenging nearby. A branch from a nearby tree suddenly extended in length rapidly enough to knock the weapon from the man's hand across the forest floor. "Set him down, *gently*, and put your hands up."

"I can't do that," the guard said with a snarl, and when his gaze met mine, I realized that I recognized him. Not in the way that I'd likely recognize any Ulmosi guard from the kingdom, but this one specifically fit a description that Zara had given me. Back on Aolan, when we had had our heart-to-heart, she had described the guard responsible for Firth's death in great detail, from his appearance and height, down to the snippy gruffness of his voice. Saar. This was that man. It had to be.

"Whatever punishment you're fearing from Ulmos, I can assure you it'll be worse here if you don't do what I say."

Evren must have heard my voice because he wiggled in the man's arms and let out a screech. My heart immediately began to race at the sound, my biological need to soothe my child kicking into overdrive. I didn't doubt that this man would harm my child in an instant, especially if he felt like he had nothing to lose. Just when I was considering the quickest way to grab my son from him, the sound of several arrows brushing against their corresponding bows filled the air; we were surrounded.

"Give the order, King Earwyn," said a voice from one of the trees. When I looked up, I realized that at least four Yannavi soldiers had made their way up into the trees surrounding our meeting point and that the captor wouldn't get far if he chose to run. They were easily camouflaged by their outfits of green and brown, which blended into the surrounding tree cover. I was impressed by their stealth and the fact that I hadn't noticed them nearby until they'd announced themselves. The last time I'd come face-to-face with them in this ready-to-attack state, they'd been turning Mycel away from the entrance of the city. It was nice to have them on my side.

I met the kidnapper's gaze again and felt hatred like I didn't know

I was capable of feeling. The sensation was so powerful, so over-whelming, that I struggled to formulate a command for my team. I was gritting my teeth so hard they threatened to crack. "Get Evren. Bring him back to his mother."

Without argument, one of the soldiers hopped down from his station in the trees nearby and approached the kidnapper. I could sense the others covering him. He stepped slowly, carefully, toward the pair.

"One wrong move," I told the captor, "and they will cut you down immediately."

He sneered, as if to suggest he knew there wasn't a right move to make at that moment. Nevertheless, he stood still, and when the soldier approached him to remove my son, who was bordering on hysterics, he didn't move. When the soldier attempted to bring my son to me, I held up a hand, knowing full well that I would crumble if I looked at the child's innocent, panicked face. "Back to the city."

The soldier nodded, but before he could turn to leave, I looked up at those other three in the trees. "Strip this man of his weapons," I instructed. "And then accompany him," I told the group, gesturing to the soldier holding Evren, "please. Make sure my son is delivered to Mycel safely."

They hopped down, two of them keeping their arrows pointed at the thief as they backed away. The third moved to the thief and stripped him of his weapons, tossing several knives, a sword, and a small flail that had been hanging from his hip onto the damp ground. When they passed me, however, one paused and asked, "My lord? You shouldn't be alone with him." I didn't know if that was for my own safety or because he was insisting that we follow the laws of the forest and bring this man to stand trial, but I waved him off. The only court this man would see was mine. In my court, we wouldn't need weapons. I would be the judge and jury. But I didn't need Mycel's soldiers around to witness it.

They didn't argue. They did as they were told, and soon they were out of earshot.

The captor eyed me curiously, then sucked his teeth as if he were in a position to pass judgment on me. His brazen confidence was astonishing, but then again, if he remembered me as the Prince of Ulmos, he only knew me as downtrodden, weak, and incapable of standing up for myself. Ineffectual. That wasn't me anymore. "They're right, you know," he said with a grunt, looking strangely proud of himself. "You really shouldn't be alone with me."

"No?" I raised an eyebrow, my fingers twitching with more restless energy than I knew what to do with. "I think we'll fare just fine."

Before we could exchange any further witty banter, the kidnapper lunged for his weapons on the ground. He was quick, but I was quicker. And when our eyes met again, I had him pinned to the trunk of a mighty western red cedar with my hand around his throat. He struggled against my grasp, trying to pry my hands off of his neck and failing. His eyes watered. My forearm strained to hold him up, his feet dangling a few inches off the ground.

I was panting. "Was it worth it? What were they going to give you back in Ulmos for all of your hard work, huh? Do you think that capturing and threatening a baby makes you tough?"

The man laughed, his dark gaze soulless and unfeeling. "No," he said between gasps. It was then that I realized he knew he had nothing to lose, that he knew the outcome would be the same no matter what he said. So he boldly, disgustingly confirmed my suspicions about who he was: "But slitting that big stupid fuck's throat sure gave me a thrill."

Before I could talk myself out of reacting, I squeezed. I squeezed so hard that the next sound in the forest was the crunch of the thief's windpipe between my fingers… and when I felt it crush, like crumpled paper, I kept squeezing. I dug my fingertips into his gills until the tissue bunched up beneath my nails, squishing and squelching.

Nothing spurred me to let go. Not the bursting of blood vessels in my hand, not the way the thief gasped and struggled against my grip, nor the scraping of his boots against the ground or the way he pissed his pants before his last remaining breaths left his pitiful body.

The forest went silent, and all that was left was my own breathing.

When I finally dropped him, he'd been dead for several minutes, his bloodshot eyes staring lifelessly through me.

I left him there.

He didn't deserve a burial. I didn't even know if it felt right to leave him for animals to eat, but I left him there like he'd left my best friend.

CHAPTER THIRTEEN

EARWYN

I had no clue how I was going to tell Mycel what I'd done.

CHAPTER FOURTEEN

MYCEL

I had run nearly five miles from the center of the city when a familiar voice echoed through the trees. "We have him!" It was a Yannavi soldier. "Maz, go tell the queen that we have Evren!" And then there was my son's cry, bright and clear, like the first day I'd met him earthside. He was alive, and my people had him again. It wasn't a pained cry... frightened, maybe, but not injured. Evren would be okay, he would be safe and secure and wouldn't ever be taken again, and my people and husband would ensure whoever had tried to harm him would be brought to justice.

I was close enough that I heard the conversation between the guard and my familiar, and my resolve crumbled immediately. I slumped against a nearby hemlock tree and gasped as if I had been deprived of air for many long, long minutes. Then, the tears came. My chest ached, pain splintering through my lungs and ribs as I slid down to the damp, cold ground. Moving had kept me busy, kept me distracted, but now that I could stop, all of the what-ifs came flooding through my mind. I trusted my people to find Evren, but there was always the possibility that they would have found him dead.

Mycel, Mycel! Are you okay? They found Evren. They found him—

My familiar's small voice drifted in and out of my head and the forest spun around me. Soon, he was on my knee, tilting his head from one side to another as I struggled to focus on his tiny, blue-black face. I gripped the cloth of my shirt as if I could reach into my chest and still my pounding heart, but no luck.

Mycel? They found— Mycel, what's going on? He's safe!

"They took him, Maz," I gasped, hot tears rolling down my cheeks. I'd been holding them in since my son's birth. Fear had followed me around like a storm cloud since the moment Evren Firth had left my body; how could I keep him safe if he wasn't attached to me? Inside, he'd been protected, he'd been fed and kept warm, and nothing could happen to him if I was safe with my body, but now… What was I supposed to do if someone could just take him from me? How could I fight if he would be a target, too? I'd pushed those thoughts as far back into my mind as I could, pushed the nightmares away once I awoke each morning, telling myself that they were a trick of my mind and that there were more important things to focus on, but— "They took him right from his crib, right next to my bed, where he was supposed to be safe! He was here, home, with our people, and someone took him!" I was panting, struggling to breathe as I sobbed my panicked thoughts to my familiar. He tilted his head again, looking as confused as a small bird could, before hopping to my shoulder and burying himself in my hair. From there, he pressed his small body close to my cheek.

But he's safe now, Mycel. He's safe. Earwyn has him. Nothing will happen to him now.

My chest heaved as we sat there. I closed my eyes and let myself lean into the warmth of Maz's head. "I should be running to him now," I choked out. "And I'm sitting on the ground feeling sorry for myself."

You'll get to him. He will be there when we get back, I promise. It's better for you to take a moment… he'll want to see you smiling, so he knows that everything is okay. And it is. It will be.

"Maz… I didn't think it could be this hard," I confessed, trying to steady my erratic breathing. "Aren't I supposed to be made for this? For childbearing and mothering? It doesn't seem right that it should be so terrifying."

I know.

I shook my head, ashamed of what I was about to tell him. "You don't know the terrible things my mind shows me when he's not right in front of me." Even if he wanted to know, it would be too much to recount, too much to put into words; it almost felt like that would make it more real.

Maz let out a chitter that sounded a bit too much like a chastising chuckle.

"What are you laughing about?" I asked him softly, eyes still closed while he rubbed his feathered head against my flesh like a housecat.

Are you forgetting who you're talking to? Of course I know your mind. Nightmares and all.

"Oh, Maz… I'm—"

And that's my job, that's part of our bond. I'll face those horrors with you… and when you're ready, you'll get up, and we'll see Evren Firth so you know they aren't real.

Eventually, we got up together and headed back toward the city to see my son and to find out exactly who was responsible for his disappearance.

CHAPTER FIFTEEN

ZARA

*M*aybe Earwyn had paired me with Reed because I'm human and he thought I needed someone with me, just in case I was the one to intercept the kidnapper; after all, how would I be able to fend off a magickal attacker? Maybe he was as worried about my fragile mortal brain as Mycel was. Maybe he was worried I'd wander off into the dark depths of the woods and disappear forever, only to become some sort of sad, lonely ghost who haunts people trying to bang during camping trips.

Whatever his reasoning, it was an uncomfortable pairing, to say the least. Reed tried multiple times to ask me questions, to commiserate about the horror of a baby being stolen, to catch me when I tripped over an unearthed tree root, but I wanted nothing to do with it. The large man navigated the woods naturally, easily, despite his size and stature, while I stumbled gracelessly through, trying to stifle my shivering so that I didn't look like a weakling. I had just considered punching the third tree to trip me when the soldier's voice blared through the woods, projecting farther than any human voice would have been able to. Did they have some sort of intercom within the trees? I imagined, for a moment, speakers built into the towering pines around us. Hmmm, probably not. The thunderous voice caused me to shiver even more. For all the warmth that Mycel insisted was in the forest, I felt cold and isolated. But the announcement caused me to stop in my tracks and exhale in relief. "Thank fuck," I groaned. On one hand, I obviously wanted my nephew to be safe. If those sea-dwelling shit-bags hurt another one of my loved ones, I'd either go insane or become Yannava's most dangerous weapon. Or both. I also sighed in relief, because damn, we needed a break. It felt like we'd been relentlessly beaten down, and the battle hadn't even begun. I supposed that was part of the enemy's war tactics.

Reed stopped, too, but a few long strides ahead of me. "That's… good," he commented cautiously, taking his time to turn around and face me as well.

I crossed my arms over my chest and looked back the way we came. "Yeah, of course." Duh. It was good that an innocent, kidnapped child had been recovered. I assumed by the announcement that he was safe and sound; anything else would have warranted a much different tone.

"Should we… head back?" Again, Reed's tone was hesitant, as if he was suddenly unsure of himself… a stark contrast between the man that had been hopping over fallen trees and attempting to rescue me at every turn.

I groaned internally. I didn't feel like making small talk, but I also wasn't eager to return to the city. "Not sure."

He looked as though he'd caught me somehow. "Oh?"

Annoyance bubbled within me. "Look, I'm glad he's safe, but I'm not itching to see the baby named after my dead lover."

Reed's eyes widened. "Your dead… lover?" The last word came out in a harsh gust. "Boyfriend" had never felt like the right title, and "soulmate" was too dramatic.

"Yeah, Firth. Rhodes's twin. Earwyn's best friend." It hadn't occurred to me that this man likely didn't know all of the internal drama of our friend group, but then again, he really had no reason to know all of those details. Even though it felt like everyone could see right through me, could see the painful memories that I had on repeat in my mind, I was reminded that most of the Yannavi had no clue who I was, where I'd come from, and how I'd gotten there. They knew I was a human friend of Mycel's, and that was enough to earn me protection.

He cleared his throat. "Oh. I'm, um, sorry. How'd he die?" He kicked the dirt with the tip of his boot, which looked to be as long as my forearm, easily. This guy was huge.

I scowled. "Also not something I'd like to relive," I told him. What kind of question was that? "And why aren't *you* eager to go back?"

Reed's eyes widened, and then he rapidly shook his head in dismissal. "Huh? I'm fine, I'm good."

"Yeah, right. You haven't taken a single step back toward the city since they made the announcement," I commented. "You'd think you'd be eager to see the newborn prince of your kingdom and ensure all is well, ya know."

Reed scratched his beard, flicking his gaze away from me before replying more honestly than I'd expected him to. "I'm not itchin' to see the baby that should've been mine, but isn't."

We stood in silence, sizing each other up through our mutual grief, different but in many ways, the same. I still didn't feel like talking, but something inside of me softened toward Reed against my will. I knew that he'd had a thing with Mycel, but I guess I hadn't understood the extent of it. By the way Mycel had described it, she hadn't viewed it as seriously as the man standing in front of me had. I could only imagine how he was feeling… It was different than the heartache of losing my requited love, but to have Mycel within reach but unavailable also seemed painful. I couldn't imagine having Firth living practically next door and having to watch him with someone else after all we had been through together. Heat rose in my cheeks at the thought.

"I didn't expect it to hit me that hard," Reed told me suddenly. I must've looked confused because he added, "Her coming back… you know, uh, married and with a baby on the way. The last time we saw each other, settling down was probably the furthest thing from her mind… and somewhere in between, she found the right person, and it wasn't me." He grunted, stifling a laugh at himself. "Look at me, pouring my heart out to her best friend. Not a smart move, huh?"

I didn't respond to his last comment. Did this hundred-year-old ethereal being expect that I would gossip like some teen? And why, to ruin my best friend's marriage? Nah. "You still love her?"

Reed laughed, then rolled his eyes a little when he looked at me again. His gaze glittered with curiosity, and his vulnerability brought me a distraction from reality I didn't know I longed for. It was painful to talk about lost love, but it was better than keeping it trapped inside of me while it gnawed at me like a termite. "You still love Firth?"

I looked away from him as if I'd been called out on a secret. "Yeah, of course." Of course I loved him. My only regret was not having told him that more to his face. It was impossible not to love Firth.

Reed's face fell and he sighed. "They're not easy people to stop loving, I'd imagine. I mean, we both know Mycel…"

"They can be amazing, and it can still be painful to think of them. It can hurt more than anything to have them out of reach," I mused aloud, partly to him and partly to myself. This was probably the most conversation I'd engaged in since our arrival in Yannava, but also since the loss of Firth. Why did I care about this man's feelings? Perhaps recognizing myself within his pain was more meaningful than I'd expected…

Reed crossed his arms across his chest. "I'm bein' ridiculous."

I backed up and leaned against a nearby tree, then slid down to its base. It was freezing. I was freezing. But it was clear we weren't going back to the city anytime soon. I shoved my hands back into the pockets of my coat and looked up at my search partner, who towered over me even more now that I was on the ground. "What are you talking about? I'm agreeing with you, dumbass."

"Dumbass? Charmin'." Reed chuckled, running a hand through his hair. When he noticed that I was bundled up on the ground, he looked shocked for not having addressed the temperature sooner and hurriedly took off his own shirt – a thick, woolen flannel – and handed it to me. He was only wearing a thin shirt underneath, and the fabric clung to his big body as if it were wet.

I tried to swat away the flannel shirt and scowled at him.

"Shut up and take it, you fragile little creature." He tossed the fabric over my front, and I hated the way an involuntary sigh of relief left me at the warmth of his clothing. God, it smelled good, too, like it had been wrapped around a pine tree. He must not have noticed, because he continued, "Yeah, you're agreeing with me, but I'm over here moaning about a lost love who is still alive and happy and here, all while—"

"You can still be sad about losing her that way, Reed," I told him, softening a little. He was mourning, too, whether or not he let himself believe it. My shivering was finally beginning to subside, despite my ass being flat on the cold ground. "She doesn't have to be dead."

He shook his head and folded his arms across his massive chest. "I'm moping over rejection."

"You're allowed to! Loss is loss. It hurts."

He was quiet for longer than I expected, and when I looked over at him, he was looking down at his folded arms.

"Reed?"

"Yeah, it fuckin' hurts," he said finally. Again, he surprised me with his willingness to just… let me in. "When she first came back, I thought I could… I don't know, charm her back into my arms, you know? Even though she was already married and pregnant. Honestly,

I probably thought that until the moment I saw the baby." He shrugged. "I've spent a good chunk of my life imagining what it would be like if Mycel had had our children, Zara, that seeing her with someone else's just…"

I cringed.

"Yeah, it's like that," Reed noted, clearly not missing my uncomfortable expression. He scratched his beard again, then laughed a little to himself as if he were still chastising himself for being sad about Mycel. I didn't know what the community was like or if he had any friends, but somehow it made sense that the universe had brought us to each other when we both needed a friend who could understand our pain.

"Sorry." I shrugged. What else could I say? I knew we both wished there was more we could do for each other, even if all we knew about the other was that they were hurting.

Suddenly, he added, "I've thought about erasin' them, my memories of her and me."

"You can do that?"

"Sure."

"Can you erase mine?"

Reed's eyes widened again, as if I were speaking blasphemy. "You don't wanna do that."

"How do you know what I want?" I scowled, wrapping my arms around my legs under his shirt and curling up against the tree a little more. My walls shot up again. Maybe we had bonded a little, but that time was rapidly coming to an end.

Reed's brow furrowed, as if he were deep in thought. For someone so bold, pushy, and according to Mycel, playful, he was able to switch to serious rather quickly. I imagined he felt the full spectrum of emotion on a regular basis if he was in charge of managing people's memories. "They're part of your story," he said finally, as if he'd been searching for just the right words to explain himself. "And some of the last bits of his, it sounds like. Someone should hold on to those."

"So? Aren't your memories of Mycel the same? Haven't they made you who you are today?"

"Not even close," Reed admitted. "She has an entire story ahead of her, and I'm just not part of it. Besides," he continued with a slight chuckle. "Do you think Earwyn wants me replaying them over and over like some lovesick parrot? Because, big shock, I do… and it drives me fuckin' nuts."

"That's none of his business."

He shook his head in shame. "It doesn't seem right. You, on the other hand… maybe hold off on trying to get rid of your memories of Firth."

"They're painful to hold on to, like grasping flames with my bare hands." I couldn't look at him when I thought about it.

"I know."

"You have no idea, dude," I told him in frustration, shocked that I was still sitting there talking about my memories, about Firth, with this man I barely knew. Hell, I hadn't even talked to Mycel about it this deeply. Earwyn and I had had our moment of connection over losing Firth, but since then I'd been buttoned up, uneasy at the idea of letting anyone, especially someone new, in.

He shrugged. "You could show me."

"I barely know you," I told him, exasperated now by his forwardness.

"And? You want someone else to feel your pain? That's my job," Reed said finally, staring at me with an intensity that didn't match the playfulness of the man I'd been talking to moments before. When I didn't respond, he crouched down in front of me and held out his hands, much like he had in the center of the city prior to Mycel's coronation. He looked like he had nothing left to lose… had Mycel's moving on really hurt him so badly? I wondered if she even knew about the depths of his love for her and the consequent pain it caused. "It's probably a good thing you don't know me." He gestured between us. "Distance."

I took a steadying breath and placed my hands in his after poking them out from underneath his shirt. They were rough, no doubt from being big and strong enough to haul trees directly from the earth, but surprisingly warm. The heat of his flesh sent a chill coursing through my chilled body, and I closed my eyes at the contact I'd been fighting for so long, not just from him, but from anyone but Mycel really, and tried to relax, but it felt like an impossible task. "What do you want me to show you?"

Reed exhaled deeply through his nose, and I could feel his gaze still trained on me. "Whatever hurts the most right now," he said; a big ask for someone I barely knew, but what did I have to lose? His breathing steadied, deepened, immediately, as if he were bracing himself. He was right to do so.

So I took Reed to the beach.

It was dark.

Firth and I had spent every evening there since Mycel had departed, hoping to catch her and Earwyn on their return from Ulmos. It was difficult to know when we might see them again with no way to communicate, so we visited frequently and tried to keep our spirits high. We often brought a blanket with us, sometimes snacks. Sometimes we built a small bonfire. Maybe it seemed careless of us to make a picnic out of it, but the more we visited without any sign of our friends returning, the more bleak it felt; we tried to keep our hopes up by using the time to connect with each other, too.

"Rhodes will help them if he can," Firth signed to me, the glimmer of city lights reflecting off his eyes. They were dark, deep, and delicious. I could stare into them forever. "Don't worry."

"What will we do when all of this is over?" I asked.

"Anything and everything, Z." My sign name again. Pain exploded in my chest at the memory, but back then, I'd been filled with love and hope. What I wouldn't give to see the sparkle in his eyes one more time; they'd been so deep and dark, like gems that only I had ventured far enough to see the true shimmer of.

"Travel the world?" I offered.

"The world, the couch, wherever you want to be, I'm there." He tangled his fingers in mine with a soft smile.

"I love you," I told him finally. That was the first and last time I got to tell him in precisely those words.

"I knew—"

A foreign voice cut him off. "On your knees."

Firth had me behind him in an instant and had turned toward the voice so that I couldn't see who was speaking to us. When he spoke, his voice was choked. Someone was pointing a weapon at him and had likely used it to get Firth's attention in the first place. "Saar, what are you doing?"

"Following orders," the voice snipped. "Something you're clearly not very good at, Firth." The other person tsk-ed, chastising my man. I wondered how much of this man's snide commentary he could actually gather in the darkness of the beach. "I really thought you knew better; no one betrays the kingdom and lives to tell the tale."

"Not here, okay? I—"

"On. Your. Knees."

"Listen, just take me back, do whatever you need to do, but leave her be. Let her leave."

"Uh-uh, both of you."

Firth's body was a wall of tense muscle. He gripped my hand hard. For a moment, I worried he would tell me to leave, to run, but when he didn't, I assumed it was because he knew I wouldn't make it. He knew what his people were capable of; I only had a slight inkling based on how he'd been left to die on our apartment floor. But if they could clear the beach or sneak up on us when we knew the area better than they did, they were probably faster than humans were. I hadn't even noticed him approach us until he was a few steps away. When he pulled us both down into the sand, the guard crouched in front of Firth and muttered something to him when they were face-to-face. I couldn't make out much beyond "humans." Firth glanced at me afterward with a look of relief on his face. Maybe he'd let us go.

The beach was emptier than it should have been, emptier than it had been every other night we waited for Earwyn and Mycel. When the surface of the water exploded with activity, Firth stared straight ahead into the distance. "Don't be afraid," he said suddenly, voice low so that only I could hear. "I love you."

"Firth, what are you—" I looked in his direction, torn between his words and the bustle of those returning from the sea, in time to see the guard drag a blade across his throat. I knew what was coming next. I'd played this moment over and over in my mind; it plagued my nightmares. But it didn't feel right to let a stranger see Firth's last moments, to let him see the light fade from my lover's eyes, or to hear his brother and best friend scream in agony when they tried to rouse his dead body. I released Reed's hands because I just couldn't go there with him or anyone else. It was horrific and painful and somehow sacred all at once.

Reed sucked in a sharp breath, as if he'd been physically wounded, and scooted away from me on the forest floor. Surely he'd seen many people live and die in the memories of others; was this all that different? Or had he not grown accustomed to it in the way that I'd expected? I wiped my face on my sleeve, sniffling loudly but not really caring how I looked. The tears finally flowed for the first time since we'd entered Yannava, and I was grateful for it… grateful to feel something other than empty hopelessness.

"Zara…" Reed's chest heaved with labored breaths, almost as if he were fighting back tears himself, and rage filled me at the pity in his gaze.

"What? You wanted to see!" I told him with a hiss.

"I did, I just… didn't expect that."

I rolled my eyes. What else was there to do? You pour your heart out to some magickal forest dude who collects memories, and he has the audacity to act surprised by you? I hoisted myself up off the ground, hoping that moving would get my blood flowing again, and headed back toward the village, but not before tossing his shirt on the ground.

"Zara, wait!"

I flipped him off and kept going. "That means 'fuck off' in human!"

* * *

REED FOUND ME LATER AND, WITH A STRAIGHT FACE, SAID TO ME, "I'M interested in getting to know you better."

"Tough shit." I tried to walk off, and he followed, much to my dismay.

"Give me a chance," he argued.

I scoffed. "Why would I do that?" I had zero desire to drag this man over to a couch for Chinese food and Westerns with the subtitles on. "Besides, you tried getting to know me earlier, and I'm pretty sure it made you cry, so…"

"People cry over sad shit, Zara." Reed shrugged. "We get what the other is goin' through. Isn't that worth something?"

"Not enough for romance, *Reed*," I said pointedly, unnerved by the fact that he used my name as if we were old friends.

"I wasn't done."

I rolled my eyes, but didn't stop him from continuing his spiel.

"We get what the other is goin' through… plus, you're, ya know, stunning, and I'm assuming you find me at least… tolerable visually?" He raised a playful eyebrow, then gestured to his body as if showing it off for sale.

I couldn't help but laugh a little, then rubbed my face in frustration. "Tolerable, sure." Anyone with eyes would agree that he was an attractive man, but I hadn't really let myself dwell on that fact. "But I don't have space for more heartbreak."

"So you know you'll fall for me, then," Reed said with a mock sigh of relief. "Glad you're being realistic."

I scoffed and rolled my eyes yet again. "Suuure, let's say I do… and then you leave or get killed in battle, then what?"

"I won't."

"You could. You might. Then that'd be a whole other annoying ordeal, and I'm just…" I sucked my teeth. "…not really in the mood. It's messy. Besides, I'm here to kick some Ulmosi ass, not fall for another giant magickal himbo."

"What's a himbo?"

"It's like…" I searched for the correct words. "A hot idiot."

"You think I'm hot?" He grinned.

"Wow, you really missed the important part of what I was saying. With my luck, your hot idiot ass is gonna get killed."

"I won't," he insisted. "And when I come out of that fight alive – scuffed up, maybe, but alive – then you'll give me a chance."

I groaned, almost angry at the way I had to stifle a smile at his bargaining. "Fine. Not a moment sooner."

Satisfied with his triumph, Reed turned to leave, but then halted in his tracks. "Hang on."

"I just said—"

"Enough arguing," he told me firmly when he turned around, the playfulness vanishing from his gaze again. "You're so damn stubborn." He shook his head, then pulled the flannel from earlier off his shoulder and handed it to me. "I can't woo you if you die from the cold – nor can you 'kick Ulmosi ass' – so you're gonna have to take this and wear it."

I took the shirt.

CHAPTER SIXTEEN

MYCEL

I returned to the village after long moments with Maz in the silence of the now-empty woods. Admittedly, I had been curious about my son's captor, but unable to pull myself from the trenches of my hysterics to get back quickly. Hell, if the thought of seeing my son didn't get me off the ground, learning about some monster who had captured him surely wouldn't.

I found my husband up in our treehouse with a Yannavi soldier stationed by our front door, as well as another inside, guarding the window opposite of the front door. Earwyn sat at the edge of the bed near the crib, his hand on our son's chest as he slept. They were probably both exhausted. I placed a hand on Earwyn's shoulder, and he flinched, almost as if he'd been in a daze, but then he put his free hand on top of mine before looking up at me. "Hey… I wasn't sure how far you'd gone. Glad you're back."

"Sorry, I… needed a minute."

Earwyn's brows knitted in concern. Meanwhile, Maz stayed on my shoulder, hovering closer than usual. "Will you tell me about it?"

"Maybe later." I gave him an appreciative nod, too shattered emotionally to meet his gaze for much longer, so I diverted my attention to our sleeping son. "Is he okay?"

"He's okay," Earwyn stated, returning his gaze to the crib as well. "A little rattled, I think, but I couldn't find a scratch on him."

Before I could respond, there was a knock at the door to the treehouse. Evren immediately roused and began crying, the sound of which accelerated my heart rate immediately. "I'll take him," I blurted out faster than I intended to, but Earwyn got the message and headed for the door. The moment my son was on my chest again, even though he was still in the midst of an exhausted whimpering, I felt like I could breathe again. Maz watched him from my shoulder, tilting his head to peer down at his little pink nephew.

See? He's okay. Hey, remember when we saw him in the water on the Spark? *Just swimming around like a little fish?*

I chuckled a little at the memory, savoring the way the little baby in my arms looked just like the child I had seen in the water. "Yeah, but—"

"Mycel." And just like that, my brief moment of peace was gone. Earwyn's voice was stern and serious, two Yannavi soldiers standing behind him in the doorway. "Hyssop is gone." In all of the chaos of retrieving Evren, we hadn't realized that Hyssop had been extracted from her holding cell. She was gone.

The shock must have been apparent on my face, because the soldiers flanking Earwyn hung their heads in shame. "They must've gotten to her when everyone was out looking for Evren," one of them stated. "I'm sorry, my queen."

"It's not your fault," I told the men honestly. I held my child a little closer as we spoke. "You went where you were most needed. This was just part of her plan. We couldn't have imagined that she'd stoop so low as to put a child in danger."

The other guard frowned. "Yes, my queen."

"Please, don't carry this with you. You all did what we needed and successfully retrieved your prince, bringing him home safely. That's what matters. His captor is behind bars now, so let us ensure that he remains there while the rest of you begin the search for Hyssop. There's no telling how far she's gotten by this point and with who."

Earwyn cleared his throat, and I looked at him nervously. "What is it?" Evren squirmed a little against my chest, and panic rose within me, but I did my best not to show it. We had to remain a united front when it came to everyone outside of our union.

He looked from me to the guard and back again. "Perhaps we should speak before you send the guards out to look for Hyssop."

When we dismissed the guards, Earwyn regarded me with a curiosity I knew to mean he was comparing his experiences in different kingdoms. "You could have torn them apart for leaving her unguarded."

I shook my head, resuming my spot on the bed with Evren, and sighed. "What good would that do? They were following our orders. We all thought the holding cell was secure enough to keep her contained while we were out looking for the baby." I tried to stifle a yawn and failed. Jitters coursed through my body, the combination of nerves and exhaustion taking its toll.

"You should sleep," suggested Earwyn.

Instead I bounced lightly as Evren finally drifted off to sleep himself, but kept my gaze on my husband. "And you should tell me what has you so nervous about the guards going back into the woods."

CHAPTER SEVENTEEN

EARWYN

"Is Elan still around? Because we might need her help to process what I've done." I scrubbed my face with my fingertips, the pure adrenaline from the day's events finally wearing off. It was then that I realized I hadn't washed up prior to coming home to my son, and the metallic tang of blood filled my nostrils. I shoved my hands into my pockets before my wife could see the evidence under my fingernails.

Mycel's eyes widened. "That's not very reassuring." Still, she seemed much more at ease than she had only hours before; it seemed that, as long as she knew those she cared about were safe for the time being, she'd be willing to scale most other hurdles. Evren was with us.

I struggled with where to begin explaining myself. "Remember how you made me promise not to kill anyone?"

"Not to kill any of *our* people," Mycel corrected. "Oh, god, Reed—"

For a moment, I felt angry at the mention of Reed. My priorities were askew. "No, not Reed. Not one of our people."

"Wyn, spit it out. You're scaring me. You can't say things like that when there are so many different terrafolk and humans involved in this... how am I supposed to know who you're including in that group or not?"

I licked my lips, which had become parched with my erratic breathing. "I was the one who found Evren and the Ulmosi guard who captured him."

Mycel held our child closer as I spoke, her bouncing never ceasing, almost as if she wanted to keep him asleep so he wouldn't hear the information I was about to share.

"And... after I made sure that Evren was safe and sent him back to the city, I dismissed the other soldiers so that I could be alone with the captor."

"Yes..."

I resisted the urge to rub my face again and forced my fingers to pinch the insides of my pockets so that they'd stay covered. "We can't send our soldiers back into the woods yet because the Ulmosi guard's body needs to be... dealt with first."

Mycel tore her gaze away from mine, and I found that I couldn't read her reaction at all, even after all the time we'd spent together. Then again, I'd never confessed to murder before. Her expression was focused, intense, as if she were processing the information, but I had no clue which way her processing was going. Was this the end? Was the return of my magick and subsequent strength going to be the undoing of our relationship? Would she be afraid of me now that I had proven I was capable of murder, just like the rest of the Ulmosi were? "Why?" I must've looked dumbfounded because when I didn't reply, she asked again, "Why didn't you just bring him back?" She looked back at me again, her brows knitted in concern. "I'm not questioning your judgment. I just want to know why. I want to understand. There must be a reason you chose that instead of instructing our soldiers to bring him back for questioning."

I gritted my teeth as I struggled to explain myself. "He took our son, Mycel."

"I know."

"That alone meant that he deserved worse than what I gave him."

My wife nodded, and the distance between us grew. "What else was there, Earwyn?"

I winced at the loss of my nickname. My throat went dry. "He… isn't that enough?"

"It's enough," she answered without missing a beat. "But I know there's more. Who was he?"

"He was the one who killed Firth, Mycel. He reveled in that fact; he was remorseless. He also took our son, and I know that if I had let him live another moment, he would've gladly done many, many more horrific things in the name of serving Ulmos."

Mycel nodded, her gaze thoughtful. I still couldn't read her expression, and her tone gave away very little. "We need to tell Zara. She deserves to know." She was right, but I wanted to stay there, in our home, and discuss this with her. I wanted to know that things were okay, that my wife didn't think I was a monster for what I'd done. But as usual, her logic prevailed when she said, "The sooner we deal with this, the sooner we can send the soldiers out again for Hyssop. They'll be awaiting our word. I'll get Clove to stay with Evren." I knew then that this was weighing heavily on her; there was no way she'd voluntarily leave our son at a time like this unless she was that concerned about the issue at hand. Even though our son was so young, I didn't blame her for not wanting him to be exposed to the disposal of a dead body. He was too young to know death, and I was thankful that he wasn't old enough to really comprehend much of what was going on around him. When the war came, I prayed that he would remain safe and secure, unaware of what was happening outside.

* * *

"Show me."

I tried to argue with Zara. "I really don't think that's—"

"Show me, Earwyn." Her tone faltered a little, and I could sense desperation in her demand. "I need to see."

I winced at her words, then looked between Zara and Mycel before relenting.

The walk through the woods was painfully silent. I led the way, of course, because I knew exactly where we were going. Even though my initial journey to find the captor had been fueled by panic and the walk back had been a blur following the first life I'd ever taken, I knew exactly where I'd left the man in the woods. When we arrived at the small clearing in which we'd pinned down the captor, I halted, suddenly unprepared to see the result of myself at full capacity. "Listen, Zara, I still don't think—"

Zara pushed past me toward the body, while Mycel stood by, seemingly unable to get closer.

The body lay still, of course, but the sight was shocking to me. Even from several feet away, I could see the bruised and battered neck of the man I'd killed, blood drying on the annihilated gills. The position of his neck seemed unnatural. His lifeless eyes stared up through the canopy. I watched Zara with bated breath, unsure of how she would process the brutal sight before her. I feared for Mycel, too, who undoubtedly wanted to see the world rid of the living scum that was Saar, but was ruled by her compassionate heart. If I were in either of their shoes, I wasn't sure how I'd react. Still, despite not wanting to be responsible for the death of another, I felt at peace with what I had done. It was necessary for the safety of our friends and family… and I owed it to Firth.

I was startled from my daze when Zara let out a blood-curdling scream into the forest air. Her shoulders heaved with sobs. "You stupid fuck!" she screeched at the body on the ground. She was trembling and looked like she might leap at the body at any moment; she was close enough to hit it, but I hoped for her sake that she wouldn't beat up a dead body. That seemed like it could be hard for a human to come back from. "I hope there's a hell for you people." She spat, her hands balled into fists at her sides. She screamed again, a wordless, guttural bellow that caused birds to flee the nearby trees. "And I hope you spend eternity there, you piece of shit!"

We all stood in silence despite the pressing need to "handle" the situation. I didn't dare look at my wife, but eventually she left her spot next to me and pulled Zara into an embrace, all while avoiding looking at the body. I kept to myself and gave them space while Mycel stroked her sobbing friend's hair and held her close. Finally, she told Zara, "He'll rot, Zara. He can't hurt anyone else now."

When Zara tore out of her arms to scream in the face of the dead body again, spitting on it in all of her rage, Mycel turned away. She caught my eye when she did so and then quickly avoided my gaze again. My chest ached.

Sometime later Zara allowed us to do what we had come to do; Mycel stood back and bent her fingers at the ground, which opened with a rumble to consume the body of the man who had killed our friend and kidnapped our son. It crawled like it was made of a million snakes until the earth had loosened, then tendrils of roots and vines and decaying leaves wrapped around the body and pulled him down below the surface of the earth like a ravenous maw. We watched until any trace of that man was completely gone and all that remained was a layer of disturbed dirt.

That was the first casualty of the war on Yannavi land.

CHAPTER EIGHTEEN

ZARA

I could hardly breathe when I took off back toward Yannava. I didn't want to be in the city or deal with people, but that was the only direction I was comfortable with alone. The last thing I needed was to wander off into the woods and run into another guard like the one whose dead body I'd just seen. When I walked, stomped, tripped over tree roots again and again, I remembered the last time I had seen that guard alive.

And then, painfully, my heart took me back to the last time I had seen Firth alive. Well, not really alive, I guess. But the last time we'd been blessed with a moment together at least.

"How long do I have you for?" I asked Firth. We had been walking hand in hand on the beach of Aolan when I stopped to sign to him; I couldn't bear not knowing when he'd be taken from me again. Would I get a warning? Would he vanish into thin air or die in my arms again? It was a shock how warm his skin felt in mine, how real he felt. It didn't make any sense to me, but I knew better than to question those few sacred moments I'd been gifted again. Even though I knew it was temporary, I felt like I myself was alive again for the first time in too long.

"Just tonight, Z." My heart shattered as he signed my name and then, in true Firth fashion, tried to comfort me. "No amount of time will ever be enough for us. But I don't know how my soul would rest without seeing you one last time, so I fully intend to enjoy every second of it." He wiped a tear from my cheek and offered me a small smile, then cupped my face in his massive hands. When he kissed me, fireworks exploded in my chest just like the first time he'd done so.

We spent the night together, and I fought so hard to stay awake, to soak up every bit of time I had with Firth, but my body had been on edge for so long that being in his arms offered me peace I never thought I'd feel again. He stroked my hair, and I listened to his heart beat with my head on his bare chest. He spoke sweetly to me until I could no longer keep my eyes open and the last thing I remembered him saying was, "Don't hide behind your grief, Z. Don't let it keep you from finding happiness again. Your story isn't over."

When the memory left me, I found that my hand was raised and pounding on the door of a Yannavi dwelling that was neither mine nor my best friend's. I didn't recall having been to this building before, then Reed opened the door with a look of pure shock across his face. He was half naked, his slacks barely hanging on his waist. His abdomen was thick and strong, with a V of muscle that disappeared into his waistband along with a trail of black and gray hair. Had he just showered? Or perhaps gone swimming with the rest of the Yannavi who were learning? I wasn't sure, but his hair was dripping onto his shoulders, where a towel was thrown around the back of his neck. And while his shock originally went to a sly smile, it disappeared quickly when he looked me over. "Y'alright?"

I shook my head a little more vigorously than I had intended. "No. Can I come in?"

"What about our deal?" He wasn't teasing me this time, though.

Instead, he seemed genuinely concerned about going against our agreement. Surely, he didn't think I was propositioning him for sex when I looked the way I did and so soon after turning him down…

"Is that a yes or a no?" I asked, suddenly exhausted from the day's events. I didn't know what had brought me to him, but there I was, worried that he'd have the audacity to reject me. Without a reply, he moved out of the doorway and gestured for me to enter.

"What happened?" he asked, rubbing the towel through his sopping wet hair. Reed's dwelling was small and simple like mine. It was also surprisingly neat, which I hadn't expected. But then again, he was kind of a surprising person.

I turned around to face him and found that the words just weren't coming. Would I give them to him if my voice would cooperate? I wasn't sure.

He grunted. "That's alright. Let me get dressed, and I'll get you some food. A drink, maybe?"

Again, without thinking, I reached out and grabbed his arm. I could barely fit my fingers around his thick wrist, and there was no way I was actually strong enough to stop him from going anywhere, but I held on regardless. He looked surprised, but stopped. "Don't," I told him, aware that his house was just as small as everyone else's and getting dressed would only involve being a few feet away. My body ached for closeness and comfort. Even a few feet would be too much for me.

Reed's brows knitted in concern, but he replied with, "Yeah, okay." He was silent when he pulled back the covers of his bed and gestured for me to sit on it. When I complied, he knelt down on the floor in front of me, still a towering beast of a man even folded in half, and took off my boots. Then he nudged me into the bed and covered both of us with a thick blanket. It smelled like him, just like his flannel shirt – which I was still wearing – had. I let myself press my body against his without any consideration for what it meant and soaked up the comfort he was offering so freely. He was warm. His deep breaths and the rise and fall of his chest lulled me into a state of safe comfort I hadn't felt in months, not even in my sleep. When his rough fingers stroked my hair, I couldn't help but cry. And, hell, I cried. They were soft, tender whimpers and single glistening, dewy tears. I sobbed, my shoulders shook, and I was certain his chest hair had become damp because of me. But he didn't care. He just kept stroking my hair, my cheek, my shoulder. He didn't stop.

"Are you gonna show me what happened?" he asked in a voice so gentle I wasn't sure it belonged to him. It was soft, but still rumbled through his chest into my ear. How many dead people had Reed of Yannava seen in his time? And since he was the ward of his society's memories dating back to its beginning, how many passed-down horrors did he have stored in his mind? Yet, still, he opened himself up to more for my benefit.

"Not today."

Reed must've nodded, because I felt his head move above me, but that was the end of that conversation and any others that evening. We lay there in silence until my trembling stopped, until our breathing synched up, and my body finally succumbed to exhaustion. When I woke, it was dark, sometime in the late evening, cool air fluttering in through the curtains of the dwelling. Reed was still next to me, and I was certain I would've frozen if not for the heat radiating off of him. His big body was sprawled out, one arm behind his head, and his face looked calm, peaceful, unlike I'd ever seen in his waking hours. I had slid out of his arms and planted my feet on the floor, hoping I could find my boots in the dark, when his tired, raspy voice said, "Don't do that…"

"What?" I couldn't bring myself to turn to him again.

"Don't leave," Reed said gruffly, shifting on the bed behind me. "You don't need to leave."

"I can't really stay."

"Why not?" He cleared his throat. "Look, I promise not to try to woo you until I prove that I can live through a war, okay? Like we agreed. Just stay… just rest some more. You're safe with me."

I was initially annoyed with the suggestion that I needed him to keep me safe, but I had to admit that my body had at least temporarily shifted out of fight-or-flight mode during my time in his house. When I didn't reply, he scooted closer on the bed and put a massive hand on my shoulder. I submitted. I rolled back toward him and let him pull me close. He buried his face in my hair, in my neck, and breathed in deep. He enveloped me. My eyes closed. My breathing steadied. I decided to stay.

"Reed?"

"Yeah?"

"Your dick is in my back."

He laughed. "You want to switch positions?"

CHAPTER NINETEEN

MYCEL

We split off following the burial in a wordless agreement that we all needed space to process. Zara took off toward the city, and Earwyn insisted that he remain in the woods for a while. We barely looked at each other as we parted ways, and while there was an ache in my heart from the rift between me and my husband, I had to get back to my son. It was difficult, painful to choose between the two of them, hell, the three of them, when I could've gone to Zara, Earwyn, or Evren for repair, but my heart told me that I had the most responsibility to the life I created. Evren Firth had spent the entirety of Clove's visit yowling as if he was in pain, and on multiple occasions I considered that his kidnapper may have poisoned him or placed some sort of hex on him. Clove assured me, however, that this was the same pitiful crying that he'd done since he was born: that of a fussy baby.

"Don't let your mind wander too far," she told me as she poured piping-hot water into a cup, brewing both of us some tea.

You'd do well to listen to her, Mycel. Maz hadn't left my side since our moment in the woods. I didn't blame him; he probably thought I was moments away from completely flying off the handle, and the repercussions of that would be bad for both of us. The way our fates were intertwined wasn't lost on me. While Maz had never had an existential crisis, I imagined it might feel as heavy as my own did right then.

I bounced, I rocked, I walked back and forth through the treehouse for as long as my fatigued body would let me. Every few moments, Clove held out a gentle hand to offer to take over, or she handed me a cup of tea or water, or forced a bite of food into my mouth as I walked by. No matter how many times I refused or accepted reluctantly, she continued with her offers unfazed. Clove had always been soft and nurturing, but I couldn't help but wonder if her guilt motivated her at all; perhaps she would not have stretched herself so thin if she didn't feel like her wife had betrayed the entire Yannavi village.

"Do you have any idea who she was working with?" I asked between bites of a simple biscuit that she'd just shoved in my face. I would have undoubtedly wasted away without my village to care for me. Evren still fussed, but it was ebbing and flowing, quieting just enough for me to hear myself think, if only for a moment. "Any idea at all?"

Clove wrung her hands, clearly unnerved by the topic. "No, I don't think so. We had an Ulmosi visitor at one point, who told us to be on the lookout for their rogue prince." Earwyn. "In the interest of keeping things civil between our people, even though they operate so much differently than us, we agreed that we would alert them if we came across him. I didn't imagine that Hyssop would tell the guards to deny you entry into your home if you came back, however… nor did I consent to her using our power as temporary stewards of Yannava to remove your magick."

I sighed, saddened at the idea of Hyssop doing all of these things behind her wife's back and even more so that I had felt abandoned by both of them when that simply wasn't the case. If only she'd known and reached out to me sooner… I swallowed the rest of the biscuit and reached out for my cup of tea before she could, holding Evren tight against my body while I bounced my leg to soothe him.

"I know you're surprised, Mycel," Clove said suddenly, her tone somber as she used a small napkin to grab crumbs off of the table before us. She was avoiding my gaze. "But I shouldn't have been. Hyssop was always… so different from me, you know. I chalked it up to the whole 'opposites attract' thing, but it often bordered on too far… and I just didn't want to see it."

"Love can do that to us…" I wiped my hand on my pant leg and reached across the table to grasp her fingers, giving them a gentle squeeze. It wasn't her fault. Clove had always seen the good in people, including me, even when I made decisions that seemed the opposite. If that was her flaw, then it was a fine one to have, I thought. She shouldn't beat herself up for the decisions of another adult, as if she had any control over Hyssop's poor choices. She was right, though; they had always been very different. Whereas Clove was welcoming and reassuring, always promising me that everything would be alright in the end, Hyssop was quick to make me face the consequences of my actions, often with very little love behind her lessons. Even in their interactions with each other, I could see Clove's graciousness in stark contrast with her wife's calculating approach. If the Ulmosi approached Hyssop with logic, they would have won her over easily. If she felt that the sacrifice of her wife and niece and even the prince to the throne was all for the greater good, she would justify those losses to herself without hesitation; if she had one admirable trait, it was how unflappable she was once she made a decision. At the end of the day, though, she was no better than Maren… and nothing like Clove.

The room went silent briefly. It was so brief, but so quiet that my body almost shut down immediately due to the lack of crying; it was ready for rest. I had Evren pressed up against my body and was patting his bottom steadily. When I realized that he was quiet and hopefully asleep, I continued the motion religiously, knowing that he would likely stir if I dared to stop. When something works with babies, you try to stick to it, I had learned… but that usually meant that they would suddenly decide it wasn't working anymore. That was exactly what happened, because only seconds later, he stirred again, rubbing his tiny face and letting out a scream that made it sound like he was being tortured. I was hitting a wall. If my brain was logical enough to believe that he was safe when out of my sight, I would've probably preferred to be interrogating his kidnapper than attempting the impossible feat of getting him to sleep for more than ten minutes at a time.

"He just won't settle!" I was so, so tired, and it outweighed the guilt I felt for being frustrated with my child. "He's been like this for days, I don't know what's wrong."

Despite having a plethora of preparations to deal with, we had tried everything in the days prior to get Evren Firth to settle. Everything. We'd walked in the woods. We'd put him in water, desperate to see if perhaps he was just missing his genetic connection to the sea. Maz had put on numerous shows, brought him treasures from the woods, and attempted to sing to him (which was really just squawking, but at that point we didn't think anything would hurt). Earwyn had crafted a swing for him, which he also hated. Zara had put him in a wrap on her back, which she said her mother had done when she was a baby; it calmed him for a bit, but then the crying started up again, and Zara was promptly done with her attempt. We walked him back and forth. We stood still. We put him in our bed. In the crib. On a pad on the floor with us next to him. I nursed him every time he made a peep. But nothing could soothe our sweet babe long enough for anyone, including him, to get some rest. Prior to the kidnapping, I had trouble letting him out of my sight, but having someone take him away so that Earwyn and I could rest was now completely out of the question. We would suffer together and die of exhaustion if necessary, but I wouldn't be able to rest without him nearby.

"Let me take him for a bit," Clove suggested, more sternly this time, getting up from the window side seat that she often occupied in our treehouse. She was so helpful when with us, but I couldn't help but wonder if she was also avoiding going back to the house she'd shared with Hyssop for so long. Hyssop... another person on my never-ending list of people to keep track of.

Let her, Mycel. You're going to lose your temper and then where will we be? You'll feel worse. Besides, she's going to be right here, in the house with him. She's not taking him anywhere. And there are still soldiers at the door. It's okay.

"You're right," I said softly. "You're right."

Clove gave me a sidelong glance, but said nothing. She didn't have a familiar, but she'd been around myself and Maz for long enough that she was probably used to me talking to him.

I pressed a small kiss to my wailing baby's forehead before passing him along to Clove, then stepped out onto the balcony to take a breath. Being responsible for others, especially tiny others, was a lot of work. Maz followed me. The door stayed open. I needed it to stay open. From outside, I could hear Clove consoling little Evren Firth, her voice drifting out of the window between his varied whimpers and cries.

"You know, your mama was a lot like this when she was a babe," Clove told my son as she walked him around the treehouse. I had stepped out to calm myself but found that being away from his noise, from the bustle of trying to calm him, allowed my mind to wander more than I liked. Soon... soon I would have to leave my son in the arms of others again, and I wouldn't know how he was doing, if he was safe, if he was scared, until I hopefully found my way back to him after the fight. What if I died? What if I never made it back? What if Yannava was desecrated in the meantime? The thought of my child, alone in a flooded forest, with no one to care for him made sickness bubble in my stomach. I took one breath, then another, reminding myself he was safe with

Clove. I let the scent of near spring in the woods fill my lungs and closed my eyes. Soon there would be trillium and dogwood and avalanche lilies filling the forest with color and new life, accompanying the lush green of pines and maples and cedar. Soon both the chill of winter and the threat of the Ulmosi would be banished from our land. I let myself find some momentary reassurance in those thoughts. Like seasons, like plants, life would change, but it could and would be for the better.

And when my eyes opened again, I caught the tail end of what Clove had been telling Evren Firth. "…that's right, we found him in a tree right outside her bedroom window, and he was squawking for her just as well. I remember his little baby feathers. He was quite the sight. Now, when I say 'baby feathers,' there were really only a couple, just little sprouts on his bald head. He was a tiny, naked thing…"

Maz squawked in indignation. *He's not gonna respect me if she tells these embarrassing stories!*

"Aunt Clove?"

My aunt snapped from her story and looked over at me, her eyebrows raised in questioning. "Yes, my love?"

"What are you talking about?"

"I was just telling little Evren about how restless you were as a baby until we found Maz. Your soul was just screaming for him, like he was for you. You probably don't remember…"

Maz flew toward the balcony just as I entered and landed on my shoulder. *You don't think…?*

"Aunt Clove, I think we're looking for Evren's familiar." I wasn't sure if they'd covered familiars in some sort of Yannavi parenting class that I'd missed, but I was willing to try anything to get my boy to relax, especially if it gave him another friend. The idea of a familiar for Evren was actually exciting; Maz would be able to communicate with whatever creature it was and keep me apprised if we were apart. I wasted no time in grabbing the woven wrap that one of my people had gifted me after Evren's birth and fastening the baby to my body so that I could take him outside with me.

"Maz, go search the trees, please. I'll scan the ground with Evren." I'd considered leaving him with Clove, but if anyone could lead us to his familiar, it was him. We just had no idea what creature we were looking for. We hit the ground nearly running, with Evren looking around as well as his infant neck control allowed him. He whimpered and whined the whole time as I delved deeper into the woods. Perhaps it would be a water creature; he was, after all, half Ulmosi. I took any positive noise from my son as a sign that I was heading the right way... a coo, a gasp, a yawn, anything that wasn't a screech of terror. Maz flew overhead, communicating to me what he found in the trees. Unfortunately, it wasn't much. Winter wasn't baby season, so wherever this creature was, if that was indeed what Evren was crying for, it would be the only one of its kind.

"Maz... I've gotta stop!"

I was panting, drained, when I slumped against a massive tree. It was unlike me to get tired like this, but then again, motherhood had presented an array of unexpected side effects.

No babies in the trees, Mycel.

"Maybe it was a foolish idea," I confessed aloud. "Maybe I'm just looking for an explanation." I looked down at the baby on my front with a sigh. "It's okay. Maybe you're just a grumpy little being."

Maz landed next to us, and I slid down the tree to the floor, then unbundled Evren Firth to nurse him. We sat in silence until I caught my breath. There had to be something to the familiar story... otherwise, why was this baby so miserable? Yannavi babies, hell, terrafolk babies, were supposed to be peaceful due to their connection with nature; the sway of the trees, the rush of water... it was all supposed to easily soothe them. I let my head fall back against the tree and closed my eyes, something I was doing a lot lately; it was almost as if I couldn't steal enough moments of rest to get through the day. Was this motherhood?

Evren was nursing quietly when a whimper drifted in my ears and caused me and Maz to look the same direction at once. It was small, barely audible over the sound of a light breeze through the trees and the rush of a nearby stream, but there it was again. My time away from the forest had clearly taken a toll on my connection to it, because I couldn't place the sound, despite my efforts. When it sounded once more, even Evren was alert and stopped nursing to look up at me with wide, blue-gray eyes. Once he was strapped to me again, we carefully sought out the noise, Maz hopping before us and tilting his head every time it chimed again.

"What is that?"

Maz chittered as we approached the stream and identified a structure of sticks near the edge of the water. It was smaller than most creature-made structures I'd seen in the stream before, but then again, familiars weren't really typical animals.

The creature called for us again, but with the baby strapped to me and the water of the stream, which was surely frigid from the winter chill, I didn't have a way to wade into the water toward the structure. I would, if I needed to, but I had to be mindful. "Maz, can you get in there?"

He trilled in confirmation.

Evren and I waited, my breath bated as we watched Maz dip into the small opening of the structure. Then, laughter filled my mind. *Mycel, it's so cute!*

"What is it, Maz? Is it safe? Can you bring it out?"

Maz chuckled to himself again. *Come on, little one, I'm going to pick you up… just to get you out of here. Believe me, you're going to want to meet your person.*

"Can he understand you?"

Think so… come on, it's okay.

When Maz landed on the bank in front of me, a small bundle of fur plopped from his beak onto the ground. I could make out the tiny webbed feet and leathery paddle of a tail before I had even crouched to pick it up, but when I had the critter in my hands, and it looked up at me, its small buckteeth sealed the deal; Evren Firth's familiar was a little beaver kit.

My son strained in his carrier to look at the little creature, and his eyes lit up once he found it. It was damp and chilly, so I tucked him next to Evren within the woven wrap, and the baby grasped him in his tiny fingers immediately. "Well, I guess that seals it."

That's pretty cute.

"Can he talk yet?"

Kind of. It's less about words and more about feelings at this point, but I think they both feel safe. I don't hear any whimpering or crying.

"I guess we'd better get these two back home. Thanks, Maz." My familiar hopped onto my shoulder and nuzzled my cheek with his slick black feathered head. I melted instantly. "What a gift for Evren to have – wait, does he have a name?"

Maz peered into the carrier, tilting his head at the beaver, who stared up at him. *Boone.*

I smiled. "What a gift for Evren and Boone to have each other."

Evren Firth slept for the whole night for the first time that evening, with his familiar curled up next to his face. The only sounds that came from the duo were small snores and whines, as if they were sharing in a dreamland adventure together. Knowing that Evren had Boone and would have that relationship for the rest of his life brought me immense peace. Maz had always been my safe place, and seeing Earwyn reconnect with Genny had alleviated so much stress for everyone; those relationships were invaluable.

CHAPTER TWENTY

EARWYN

spent a lot of time staring at the lumpy ground where Mycel had buried Saar. I could've used that time to look for Hyssop with the guards or teach the Yannavi to swim or do anything but what I actually did. Instead, I stared at the ground and wondered what the earth would do with the body of the man I killed; despite his malice while living, his body would nourish the soil, feed creatures, perhaps. I thought Zara would've gotten some closure from what I had done, that Mycel would've been understanding, but none of that had happened. What really came of my decision was distance and confusion. Despite my magick and renewed healing powers, my hands ached from strangling the Ulmosi guard. His blood on my fingers was so dark I wondered if it would stain them forever. It would be fitting that I should walk around with a reminder of what I had done and just how like the Ulmosi I was.

Before I could step foot into the treehouse I shared with my little family, Genny had sped out onto the landing to alert me. First, she warned me, the baby was sleeping, so I needed to be very quiet. She knew well just how difficult it had been for us to get him to settle.

Secondly, he was only asleep because Mycel and Maz had found his familiar: a small beaver kit named Boone. Normally that would've been a topic to celebrate, and I would have loved to hear all about the discovery of Boone, especially because I didn't remember much about meeting my own familiar as a small child... but the tone of the day was not one that supported that kind of merriment. I had killed a man, and now I had to face the consequences of that decision.

"You're afraid of me," I told my wife when I stepped into the building, trying to keep my voice low, but still needing to clear the air as soon as possible.

Mycel shook her head before turning away from our son and his familiar, who were resting peacefully in their now-shared crib. Maz was perched on the edge of the crib, his body fluffed up into a ball as he slept along with them. Just when we had solved one issue, another arose; our son was safe and finally sleeping, but I had literally killed a man. What a trade-off. "No, that's not it."

"Are you sure? Because you haven't looked me in the eye since I told you what I've done, and, Mycel, I can't stand this. There should never be fear in our relationship, and here I've brought it in." My voice cracked, against my will. Great.

When she closed the physical gap between us and placed her hands on my chest, I closed my eyes. It felt like forgiveness. "I'm not afraid of you," she insisted, stroking my chest through the fabric of my shirt. "I'm just afraid of what this means for us." She was looking up at me intently when I opened my eyes again, as if to prove that I was wrong.

I opened my mouth to argue, to question her phrasing, but she put a single finger over my lips to silence me. She was so close that I could smell her, and I wanted nothing more than to feel like our union was safe and comfortable again, despite my repeated fuck-ups.

"Not for our relationship," she corrected.

Another sigh of relief.

"But war means death, murder. I suppose I knew that, especially since we lost Firth, but I had never considered that lives would be ended by us," she said thoughtfully, breaking our eye contact and looking at her hands. She continued fiddling with the fabric of my shirt as she mused aloud. "I understand why it happened and why it will happen again, but it's hard for me to wrap my head around… hard for me to be okay with."

"You don't need to be okay with it," I told her. "I'm not okay with it. Just because we acknowledge that injury and loss are inevitable in war doesn't mean we're… complacent." I put my hands over hers and stroked her soft, freckled flesh. "I suppose I'd be more concerned if you weren't upset."

Mycel leaned against me, placing her head on my shoulder with a sigh. "I'm not upset with you. I just want this to be over quickly," she confessed. "It feels like we've been fighting this fight for so long that I don't even know what normal life could look like for us."

I kissed her head, then rested my cheek against it. "I know."

"Tell me what it would look like, Wyn. Tell me what it's going to be like when this is all over."

I released my wife's hands and pulled her over to our bed, where I instructed her to lie down. She complied. Then, I stripped myself of my bloodied shirt and scrubbed my hands clean in the small wash basin of our tiny home before joining her. It didn't feel right to bring the literal blood of our enemies into a place as sacred as our bed. Evren and two of the familiars continued to snooze quietly; Genny was out chasing critters through the forest, most likely. Yannavi guards still remained stationed at the entrance of our home, as well as on the balcony. When Mycel curled up next to me and put her head back on my chest, I settled in with her and closed my eyes.

"Let's see…" I began. "Evren will grow up, probably faster than we expect. He'll have friends here in Yannava." It took great effort for me to imagine what that would be like, what our life could be like.

Living in the human world together had been a front. It had been enjoyable because we were together, but we weren't human, and we couldn't live authentically there. Not to mention the fact that we'd been hiding ourselves from each other the whole time. Now was our chance to really explore what things could be like for us in their full potential. "Maz will start his collection again. The forest will be safe for you to explore in, to adventure in alone or with our people, and to nourish."

I told her all of the thoughts that came into my head until we both dozed off, only waking again when our son stirred from his nap. Mycel responded to Evren's whimpering with alarm, sitting upright immediately before turning toward the crib. It took her a moment, but when she realized that Evren was still there, safe and sound next to Boone, who was yawning in response to his disrupted sleep, she let out a deep breath. "It's okay," I reminded her. "He's safe."

CHAPTER TWENTY-ONE

MYCEL

"So, how does it work? You just find a baby animal nearby, and then it's your best friend? Why doesn't everyone have one? Not that many people on Aolan have them. Well, Aunt Anala did. What ever happened to Ember? Aunt Anala never really told me about Ember." Neeri asked this all the next day, fawning over the tiny beaver and his human counterpart. We sat on the balcony of the tree-house and had been discussing plans to prepare the Yannavi for the impending flood, because that seemed to be a sure thing, despite their original attempt to beat us failing. Well, we were trying to discuss it, at least. Neeri looked at her dad and continued her stream of questions without stopping to take a breath. "How did she get Ember? Where is Ember?"

When she stopped, Zahir exhaled sharply as if he'd been holding his own breath. "That's a lot of questions. How do you have so much energy? Did those Yannavi kids give you some weird forest snack?" He chuckled a little to himself. I knew he was joking, but I hoped for Neeri's sake that no one had given her anything too adventurous; there were a number of questionable plants and fungi in the forest that could have concerning side effects if not handled with care. With any luck, they'd just given her something very sugary…

"Ember is back on your island," I told Neeri, thinking about the fiery little newt that had traveled in my sleeve for a while. I hoped that she was okay, but I hadn't heard many positive tales of familiars living after their people had passed. "As for how they're created… or selected…" I mused aloud, unsure of the correct wording, "it's a little more complicated than that, I think… But I guess I don't really know all of the details."

"I might," Earwyn chimed in, scratching behind Genny's ears while he spoke. She was curled up on his lap, asleep. It always warmed my heart to see them together, especially now that they could communicate again. I shuddered a little when I remembered the empty darkness of being unable to talk to Maz. "Or I at least know the lore behind it. Hard to say how much of it is true, because none of us really remember finding our familiars, since it was so early on in our lives."

"But how do you know there's one out there for you?" Neeri continued, practically buzzing. "What are the chances that your familiar just happens to be nearby when you could be anywhere and they could be anywhere—"

"Right," Earwyn began again, attempting to slow the girl's stream of consciousness. "Well, terrafolk babies are usually pretty placid, Neeri." Earwyn looked at Zahir. "Wouldn't you say?"

"Oh yeah, she never cried, at least not for long," he responded with a shrug. "If she was upset, I could take her out to look at the ocean or sit by the fire and she'd settle."

Zara smirked from her seat at the table.

"Not always the case with human babies, or so I've heard," I chimed in.

Earwyn nodded. "Sometimes a terrafolk baby might be particularly hard to settle, fussy, sad, miserable, uncomfortable. Obviously, they can't speak, so it's hard to figure out what's wrong, but in some of those instances, it's because they're missing their familiar."

Neeri pressed on, but we were all just as curious as she was. "But why, how do they get chosen?"

"That, I have no idea. But the idea is that when these specific terrafolk, like Mycel, Evren, and myself, are born, their soul..." He paused, searching for the right word. "Kind of pops, like an ember exploding away from a crackling fire, and part of it – the ember – lands somewhere else, in an animal. Without that animal by their side, they're incomplete... and well, that soul-split is why familiars are born on the same day as their folk and why the two feel so lost without each other."

"I don't think anyone really knows how terrafolk are chosen to have a familiar," I mused aloud.

"Maybe the universe just knows that some of us need an extra companion." Earwyn shrugged, looking down at his otter friend. I wondered what they were talking about in their own secret familiar way.

"Knowing how much they mean to you makes this harder, but..." Zahir chimed in, looking from me to Maz. "I think you need to send Maz up to the rest of the Alaskans. It's the fastest way for us to get a message there, and we're going to need them soon."

CHAPTER TWENTY-TWO

ZARA

Tagging along with Mycel and Earwyn on this adventure that just happened to be their life was wild and crazy and interesting all on its own, but by far the most iconic moment of our time together thus far was the arrival of the Alaskans. I mean, "the Arrival of the Alaskans" sounds like a pretty big deal just from the name alone, right? Well, the other Alaskans, since half of them were already with us by that point. Mind you, I hadn't met these ones, because I had been stuck on the island with Earwyn and Rhodes, wallowing in self-pity, when Mycel went to meet them, but I knew that if they were anything like their already-present counterparts, they were going to be cool.

I just didn't know exactly how cool.

When five colossal polar bears came lumbering into the central forest clearing of Yannava, one of them with a young woman on her back, I was awestruck. I'd never seen a polar bear that close up, aside from one sad and thin creature at the zoo. These were different… they were robust, with fur that looked soft enough to bury your face in. Their noses and eyes were glossy black, and as they breathed, they filled the late winter air with gusts of condensation. The girl on one of their backs was stunning, with white-blond hair that seemed to catch the breeze just right; it almost looked like she was moving in slow motion. The ground trembled with the weight of the bears' paws, which were easily as long as my arm, and each of their steps left a clear footprint in the softening, damp ground. At the top of each footprint were divots where the massive claws of each foot dug into the ground, and I shuddered at the thought of being on the receiving end of a swipe from one of those paws. They could gut you in an instant. How. Fucking. Cool.

Get this, though: not only was the girl riding on the back of one of the polar bears, she had a falcon sitting on her shoulder… and that damn falcon, it was like the breeze was blowing through its feathers, too. That must have been how Maz was able to communicate with them; he followed close behind, soaring into the village and finding his person with ease as the rest of the Yannavi welcomed their new guests. I saw Mycel's shoulders relax a little when Maz landed next to her, and in turn, I felt a small bit of relief myself. If she ever lost that bird, there would be hell to pay… even more hell than there already was.

It was then that I decided there needed to be some sort of honorary magickal position for humans that got pulled into terrafolk dealings. I'd have to ask Mycel if she could give me a cool power or let me turn into a tiger or something. Or maybe I'd at least get a neat animal friend? Maybe I could partner up with one of these bears, though I had no clue what they were like in their human form. If Rhodes was any indicator, awesome animals didn't always equal awesome people.

Before they could be formally welcomed by Mycel or Earwyn or patted down by the Yannavi soldiers, the crowd broke so that Owen, Nora, and Thatcher could greet the rest of their family. Owen immediately threw an arm around the neck of one of the bears, ruffling its yellow-white fur and patting it on the back like an old friend.

Nora, meanwhile, fussed over each of "her boys" and "her little girl" while Thatcher helped his sister down onto the forest floor. It was truly a sight to behold… hell, if I told anyone outside of this world what I'd seen, they'd have me locked up for my own safety, I'm sure. Their reunion made my heart ache for my own family.

Sometime later, the bears had all turned into their human selves and were making more of a ruckus than Yannava had seen in weeks, aside from the original celebration of Mycel's crowning. They were a rambunctious group and must've been used to shifting around other people, because they didn't seem to care that they were naked in public until Mycel encouraged them to put pants on. They picked on each other and laughed and teased and in moments of rough-housing would push each other so hard that they'd bump into trees and nearly knock them free from the ground.

Firth would've loved them.

I watched quietly from the sidelines while they talked and planned with Mycel and Earwyn over dinner, which they ate eagerly and with no regard for their manners; they weren't rude, in fact, they were exceptionally gracious and thankful, but almost all of them licked their fingers cleaned and forwent utensils. Even the Alaskans that had already been with our group seemed to open up more and become a little more feral when surrounded by the rest of their family. In a way, it was nice to see the contrast between them being without each other and all together.

And Rhodes, Rhodes did love them. In another life, he might have been one of them: big, loud, outgoing, and a bit destructive, though not intentionally. I supposed being a bit of a hazard just came with the territory when you had the ability to shift into a giant predatory animal. He was more hardened than the bear family, perhaps a little less tactful, but overall they seemed made for each other. Where they were lighthearted and jovial, Rhodes was snarky and sarcastic, but he seemed to soften around them.

Somehow the girl, Agnes, was very obviously part of their group, despite being the complete opposite. Her brothers joked with her and poked at her, and she took it all in stride. But the second she left the group, they each seemed to take turns keeping their gaze her direction, as if to ensure her safety at all times. Her falcon, Oona, worked in unison with the boys to keep her person safe. From the outside, it was clearly fueled by love, yes, but Agnes was obviously harboring something special that they wanted to protect. She was small, thin, but the energy surrounding her was colossal, bigger than all of the bears combined. What hell would she rain down upon the Ulmosi when they arrived? I couldn't wait to see.

Reed, meanwhile, watched me while I watched them. I tried to avoid his gaze, because every time we looked at each other, he winked or grinned at me. It made my heart flutter, whether with intrigue or irritation, I couldn't tell. I hated it, and I really, really wanted to hate him, but I didn't. I couldn't. Every time I wanted to retreat within myself, he caught my eye, and something bloomed inside my chest. When I pulled the collar of his shirt up a bit around my neck for warmth, a triumphant grin crossed his face. Jerk.

"I'm cold," I mouthed across the table.

He rolled his eyes. "Sure."

I slept in his arms again that night.

SPRING

CHAPTER TWENTY-THREE

ZARA

The attack from Ulmos came in waves. Of course it did, because they're from the ocean. Waves. Ocean. Get it? Ugh, assholes. I don't know much about war, but it seemed like they were trying to thin us out over time so that we'd surrender… or for some final boss type fight. Either way, it was hard to keep calm when every body of water in the forest overfilled and began flooding the ground around us. It happened so quickly that I woke one morning to over a foot of water in my dwelling and the sounds of many Yannavi scrambling to get out of their own homes. When I scrambled to grab the last few belongings that I could call my own, my heart sank a little: another home gone.

Thankfully, the day before had been spent primarily equipping those who could fight. The Yannavi's ability to crank out armor with their magick was impressive. They even took care to tailor each suit to the person it was for; for me, they had imbued the intricate armor with as many magickal properties and protection as they could pass on to a human. The Yannavi armor looked to be made of tree bark; it had the same ribbed, gnarled appearance and was light, which made it easy to move in, but I found that each piece was nearly impossible to penetrate. Earwyn had been gracious enough to teach me to wield a shortsword, which was certainly a skill that I hadn't imagined picking up back when I lived in Seattle. Then again, if there's going to be a rogue human wielding a sword, you'd probably find them downtown.

We had trained for hours that day. The Yannavi soldiers who were not busy monitoring the perimeter of the city aided Earwyn's efforts by training other terrafolk how to wield weapons, which was a novel idea to many of them as well. Our guests also joined; the Alaskans, most of whom decided to forgo armor and weaponry so that they could shift easily between their two forms, as well as Rhodes and Zahir. The most impressive of all of the weaponry belonged to Zahir. I hadn't gotten the story behind it, but some of the Yannavi craftsmen had created a leather brace for one of his arms that had multiple buckled straps. Those straps held the handle of an ax in place, allowing him to swing it viciously without having to grip the handle. Neeri begged for a "cool" suit of armor like my own and insisted that she could protect herself, but at every turn the adults (myself included) reminded her that she would not be fighting. She would have an equally important job, however.

The rest of the group had cleared out for the evening when I finally had the courage to bring up a question I'd been harboring for months. "Who is responsible for Firth's death, Earwyn?" I asked suddenly, knowing that if I didn't get it out then, I never would. I needed to know all of the reasons I was putting my life on the line during this fight, and I needed to know that, even if I died, I had the ability to leave a mark on my way out. "I mean, I know the guard was the one who did it, but who ordered it? I'm guessing you know."

The corner of Earwyn's mouth quirked up into a small smile: a rarity for me to witness. He sheathed his own sword and looked me up and down, a glint of pride in his gaze. "You out for revenge?"

"You better fuckin' believe it."
"I'll be right behind you."

CHAPTER TWENTY-FOUR

MYCEL

The first wave was swift, and the water level in the forest rose rapidly overnight, just as the first whispers of spring had crept into Yannava. When we woke to the sounding alarm of the Yannavi guards, the people sprang into action according to our plan. My first order of business was getting Neeri and Evren settled into one of the highest, most secure treehouses, along with several others who would not, or should not, be able to fight. Despite her brave face during our weeks of preparation, Neeri looked terrified as I handed my son to her. "It'll be okay," I assured her, tucking a blanket around Evren. Boone, whom I'd plopped into my pocket while gathering Evren and all of his belongings, wiggled to remind me to return him to his person. I took the small creature out and put him on top of Evren, where he settled in next to the baby's face. The little creature let out a small squeak. "We'll be back before you know it… you'll be safe here."

"Keep my dad safe, please," she said finally before I turned to leave, terror in her eyes.

"I will." I thought of her aunt, who had died a violent and terrifying death at the hands of the Ulmosi court, and vowed not to leave this child without her parent. I stroked the young girl's cheek and tucked a strand of dark hair behind her ear.

"Wait, what do I feed him? What if he cries?" Neeri asked suddenly, her youth and inexperience suddenly very obvious. She was just a child. I was asking so much from her. Too much, but there was no changing the plan now. They were coming.

I swallowed hard, realizing just how unprepared I was. Yannava wasn't like the human world. We didn't have breast pumps or refrigerators or bottles… and while Neeri's question was fair, I hadn't been expecting to be away from my baby for so long that he'd have to eat. "If he cries, just talk to him. Boone will help keep him calm. If he's hungry… Maz will keep an eye out, I'll get you milk somehow." I shuddered at the thought of attempting to fight with the ache of engorged breasts and even more so when I imagined expressing milk into a container for my baby while arrows and swords flew past me, but I would do what I needed to. "There are soldiers stationed down below you," I told her. "But this is for you." I unbuckled a small dagger and sheath from my hip and set it down next to Neeri, praying that she wouldn't need it. It was old and plain, a simple weapon that I had crafted myself as a young woman, but it was sturdy and sharp. If the Ulmosi got far enough that she had to unsheathe her new weapon, all was probably lost, but I was desperate to give her some peace of mind.

I cast one last glance at Neeri and Evren and at the other small children holed up in the treehouse along with some elders and another single guard that we had appointed to guard the entrance to their dwelling from the inside, then forced myself to leave.

The water rose so quickly that even Earwyn was surprised by the sheer depth of the water surrounding the trees, and despite our preparations, it led to almost immediate destruction. Blooms barely lifting their sleepy heads from the shelter of their buds were squashed, ripped from the ground by the tide, and carried off, never to take root again. The trees that were too weak to hold their ground were felled by the soft ground, which loosened their roots' hold on the earth; they hit the surface of the water with loud slaps, then floated away, leaving animals scrambling to stay atop them as their homes became water-logged. Many of us tried with all our might to will our magick into the roots of these trees, but it was no match for the rushing current of water, which seemed acidic in its destructive nature, so we abandoned the smaller trees for sturdier ones. Because we didn't know what lurked in the water, we decided to avoid it at all costs. The memory of the liopleurodon still lurked in the shadows of my mind, its all-seeing eyes and razor-sharp teeth haunting my dreams.

The devastation throughout the forest was very real and very heavy. That, in and of itself, was enough to make our people feel like defeat was imminent, but the water also overtook the homes of every single Yannavi who had built a dwelling on the ground; there were so many that it hurt to think about. Earwyn and I scrambled to pull every Yannavi up into stable trees, up into the treehouses, and to safety, but the destruction below was hard to look away from. Everywhere we turned, the belongings of our people floated by in the rushing water below: clothing, furniture, the bouquets families had kept on their kitchen tables, toys that parents had hand-carved for their children… the entire livelihood and history of some of these families had been washed away. I told myself again and again that those could be replaced, that stories could be rewritten, if we protected the lives that they belonged to.

The polar bears were hard at work getting people off the ground and up into the trees, particularly those who had not shown an affinity for swimming. There were only a few left when Thatcher was the last one in the water, transporting a young father with a small child strapped to his back. Earwyn had mentioned him; the young man, Sylvan, had been a fine swimmer, but his son had panicked at the sight of water, despite their attempts to at least acclimate him to the small rivers within the woods. Sylvan had tried and tried to get his son across the water to his assigned spot until Thatcher found them and offered to transport them, for which the young father was beyond grateful. He had just found his footing on the tree when Thatcher let out a rumbling growl and moan.

"Thatch!" Owen called from a tree several yards away, where he had turned back into his human form and was climbing up onto the platform toward his clothing and some of the other bears. "What is it?"

The bear hissed in pain, and from where I stood, I could see the fur on his sides almost sizzling in the water.

"Get him out!" I yelled. "Get him out of the water, it's burning him! Earwyn!"

The people in the tree above Thatcher threw a rope down, the edge of which immediately began to deteriorate upon hitting the water. Even so, Thatcher couldn't seem to get himself close enough to the tree to reach the rope, nor could he shift back to his human form to reach for the rope and climb in. He yowled in pain.

"Thatcher, you gotta get closer!" Earwyn yelled as he began to climb down toward the bear, struggling to do so.

Before he could reach him, there was a loud splash, and Owen had thrown himself off of his own tree into the water next to his son. He grunted and groaned as the poisoned water bit at his flesh, but stifled his own cries of pain, which were no doubt building up inside him. His pale, furred flesh turned pink and spotted with droplets of blood as he swam toward his son.

"Come on, Thatcher, let's go," he grunted, grabbing the young man by his fur and hoisting him under his arm.

The two paddled toward Earwyn, who clung to the base of a tree only inches from the water with the rope secured around his waist. He reached out with a free hand toward the two Alaskan men. From where I stood, I could see him wince when the older man grabbed his arm, the water affecting even him. I wondered how the Ulmosi would stand it themselves, but they probably had access to some sort of protectant that Earwyn and Rhodes didn't inherently have. He pulled them up with a mighty heave and somehow, miraculously, held Owen to his chest while Owen held on to his son. Above them, the other Yannavi pulled the three men up to the platform.

On the way up, Thatcher changed back to his human form, but he was limp, his flesh burned just like his father's.

Genny watched intently from the platform as the others pulled the men up to inspect and help them. Maz tilted his head toward their tree as he listened in for messages from her.

They're alive, he told me. *But they can't fight. They need to go up with the others. Thatcher doesn't look so good. Earwyn doesn't know exactly what they've done with the water, but Genny thinks she's heard of it before.* He didn't wait before flying off to find the rest of the Alaskans, no doubt to inform them of their relatives' status through Oona.

My head spun, and helplessness overwhelmed me. It had only been a matter of minutes, it seemed, and already so many of us were injured. The wailing of a small Yannavi child set me on edge, despite knowing that my own was safe. Evren was up high, with Neeri. He was safe. He wasn't near the water.

I looked toward the noise, unable to focus without seeing for myself that it wasn't Evren Firth and that whoever it was, was safe. There I found the little boy from earlier, not too much older than my own son, strapped to his father's back as the man got them to a platform in one of the trees. The little boy was leaning far away from his parent's body, reaching down toward the water where a little stuffed creature was being carried away by the rushing water. "Be-ah! Papa, be-ah!" he screeched, his tiny hands grasping at the air.

"No bear," his father told him, panting as he hoisted them up into a group of our people who helped the pair with open arms. They pulled the man and his son further onto the platform and away from the edge so that they were safe, even with the baby's intent reaching. "I'm sorry, but we have to leave him. It's not safe. Papa will make you a new bear."

My heart ached. The baby soon became inconsolable, wailing and thrashing, and though I couldn't see his face, I could imagine it ruddy and wet with tears. "Be-ah! Be-ah!" Maybe this little one didn't have a familiar, and the tiny stuffed bear, already ragged from months of love, was his only comfort. I watched as it floated on the foreboding surface of the water, seemingly unaffected by whatever was plaguing the flood; perhaps it was only made to harm flesh and fur and other organic matter?

I stood on a platform several trees away from the little boy and his father, who was desperately trying to console him and quiet him as we waited to see what was coming next, when Maz flew overhead, surveying the water below. *I'll get it.*

"Maz, don't!"

Any other time, it would've been fine to snatch up a dropped toy from a screaming tot. But not this time. Before I could stop him, my familiar swooped toward the water to pick up the stuffed toy in his beak. It was as if the forest went completely silent as his black silhouette dipped down, so close to the surface of the water. How he didn't notice the colossal shadow beneath the surface, spanning at least twelve feet, I wasn't sure, but the air seemed to shift as he approached it. Just as he grazed the fabric of the toy, the surface of the dark water exploded with activity. The slim head of another prehistoric beast broke the surface of the water, and my blood ran cold as it leaped for Maz, grabbing him by a tail feather before flopping its horrific body into the water again. It disappeared into the water again but not before gnashing its mouth, which was lined with rows of jagged teeth. Where the Ulmosi sourced their extinct, prehistoric henchmen from, I had no idea. The water sloshed and splashed, the bases of trees around it sizzled with the impact, and for a second, I lost sight of my familiar.

I screamed, horrified at the idea that, after all we had been through, this was how my familiar and I would be separated: over a stuffed animal. Just like my horror when I'd been confronted with the fact that war meant death, I was struck by fear and misery when I realized that some of that death could be my loved ones. "Maz!"

The crow screeched, his rescued toy falling from his beak as he did so, and flapped as hard as he could to get away from the water. I remembered to breathe only when I realized that Maz had escaped, one feather less – which fluttered down back to the water sadly – but still alive, and was hurriedly flying back toward me. The bear was gone, but my familiar had made it. He was too panicked to send me any clear thoughts, but I kept my gaze on him when the surface of the water rippled again. Either there were more, or the single halisaurus was a tenacious little bastard. We needed to get rid of it; between the water being uninhabitable and the voracious beast lurking beneath it, our chances of success were looking bleak.

"Archers, take it down!" my husband's voice boomed from a platform nearby, where he was directing a fleet of archers perched throughout the trees. "Now!"

Maz resumed his spot on my shoulder, his chest heaving and feathers fluffed in panic, just as arrows hailed down toward the water. "Don't do that again," I scolded him, trying to catch my breath. "You're more important than a toy bear. That little boy will survive without it."

Don't worry, if we go down, we go down together.

That sentiment didn't seem quite as romantic now, when both of us meeting our untimely end was a distinct possibility. I swallowed hard. I did not feel brave nor fearless as I stood there, staring into the flooded wasteland of my home, where our people were already falling. And what was the count? We'd only taken down one Ulmosi, and that was before the fight had actually begun. My stomach turned.

The Yannavi archers kept their arrows coming as the halisaurus rose from the water and then submerged again, disappearing from sight. Each arrow that hit the body of the beast simply bounced off of it and fell into the water, where the wood sizzled and crumbled upon impact; our weapons weren't working.

I had turned toward my husband to exchange looks of horror when the tree holding myself and several others between the platforms and treehouses on it shook.

It's ramming into the tree.

I had to act quickly. "You," I commanded, pointing at a group of younger Yannavi men who were standing at the ready with their swords, "keep the roots strong."

The archers continued their attempts to bring down the monster with no luck, and it felt like the battle would be ending much sooner than I had anticipated. "Stop!" Earwyn yelled finally. "Don't waste your arrows!"

Trees all around us were filled with our people, our friends, our family. Far off in the distance I could see the stark white-blond hair of the Alaskans and Rhodes standing with them. Zahir and Reed stood staring out from another platform, ensuring other people stayed behind them while they surveyed the flooded grounds below. There was no way to know what they were thinking, what they were planning; none of what we had originally planned had accounted for this so far. Sure, we'd gotten our people out of the water, but for what? Just to corner them in the trees, which the Ulmosi could certainly climb, for easier slaughter?

The little boy wailed a few trees over, crying for his bear still, and I wished that was the biggest of our worries.

CHAPTER TWENTY-FIVE

EARWYN

What had we, a group who was not seasoned in battle or war, expected to come of our face-off against one of the most violent groups of terrafolk on the planet?

Behind me, Thatcher groaned as he was hoisted by his injured father and several soldiers up higher into the treehouse above us. He had barely opened his eyes as we pulled him up into the tree, and while our people had lifted us via rope, I had witnessed some of his flesh slough off. Nora was, no doubt, beside herself as she stood by with her other boys and Agnes.

The dinosaur threw its body against Mycel's tree again, once, twice, three times, until the water surrounding it was tinged with its vile blood. It didn't shriek or withdraw, just kept pounding away as if it was programmed to deal blow after blow, regardless of the cost to itself, and it probably was. If the Yannavi weapons were no match for this beast, I doubted that Rhodes and I could gang up on it like we had done with the liopleurodon on the *Spark*. Not only were the weapons an issue, but I didn't think Rhodes was immune to whatever was in the water. Just when I felt like I was running out of ideas before we'd even truly begun, an unfamiliar noise sounded from somewhere high up in the canopy.

It was a trumpeting sound unlike anything I'd ever heard, and when I looked for it, the familiar uniform of the Aolani army peeked out from the tops of the trees. Leading their group was the stocky man who had made our time on their island less than pleasant: Ossian. He looked down his nose at me with a glint in his gaze that told me he was more confident in their weaponry than I was in ours, and he raised a hand, to which many of his people responded by pulling their arrows against their bows. It happened all at once, in unison, with a sound that vibrated through the foliage. When his hand dropped, all of their arrows flew at once, and with stunning precision, nearly all of them speared the dinosaur, which had not relented for even a moment. The screech that sounded through the air was horrific, a splitting echoing howl as each arrow pierced its hide. From my vantage point, that seemed like enough to still the beast, and yet... I looked up at Ossian again.

He gestured back down to the beast in the water, where it writhed just beneath the surface. It began to glow, the tip of each arrow burning bright until it caused the beast to burst into flame from the inside. It took a moment for it to combust, and then it was nothing but a floating carcass, drifting lazily in the flooding waters below.

I gave the man a nod of appreciation.

CHAPTER TWENTY-SIX

MYCEL

The collective sigh of relief as the halisaurus was taken down could be heard throughout the trees. I glanced at the tree-house in the far distance which housed my son and Neeri and so many other delicate beings. They were still safe. It felt impersonal for Ulmos to send a beast to do their bidding, to die for them without them having to witness its suffering. I liked to think that we would not have stooped so low even if we had such powerful creatures at our disposal in the forest. As much as I wanted our fight to be over, I also wanted to see the faces of those who were attacking us. I wanted to see Maren. Hyssop. This was not simply two warring nations fighting for resources or land or control; this was personal. It was intimate, even.

Only a few moments passed before the ground rumbled again and the water below twisted and turned and wriggled with what turned out to be at least ten more halisauruses.

"Aolani!" came Ossian's call. That was all he had to say, and the arrows flew again, fiercely accurate and deadly. My stomach turned when each new dinosaur joined the initial attacker and went belly up in the water, staining it red as far as the eye could see. The sun was setting, too, and reflected off of the crimson water. The smell of sopping, decomposing organic matter mixed with the sick metallic tang of blood. We all watched the water with bated breath, wanting to ensure that no creatures remained lurking below that could continue to push at the trees, or worse, lunge at someone who ventured too close to the water. But it was getting dark and difficult to see.

When the sun had finally set, the Aolani used their magick to light torches on the platforms of each tree, allowing us visibility into the suddenly frightening woods. Not once before had I related the dense woods with fear, but war had the ability to change our view of many things.

Unsure of what the next day would bring, we spread the word to set up shifts amongst ourselves, with half of each group retiring to their tree's dwelling for food and rest while the remaining half stood watch. Every familiar stayed near their person in case they were needed to deliver messages. When the Aolani shuffled amongst the trees, I was amazed by their climbing style, which was so different from ours; our people used the trees like ladders or rock walls, grabbing branches and leaves and knots to use as hand- and footholds, whereas the Aolani scaled each tree with a shuffling motion. They each had a length of rough rope with them that they threw around the trunks to shimmy their way up, no doubt due to their history of climbing branchless trees. They were shockingly adept and moved quickly. Because of this, they were able to help people move from tree to tree if they were willing to hold on to one of their backs. The Aolani helped Nora get back to her husband and one of her sons so that she could tend to them, while the other bears and their younger sister all stayed in a group.

Meanwhile, Zahir was able to make his way back to Neeri to check on both her and Evren. I knew he had made it when Boone communicated with Maz, who was back by my side.

They're okay. Your son is hungry.

"I'm coming." I ensured the safety and shifts of the people in my group before making my way through the trees. I was good at it, sure, but I was nothing like the Aolani in terms of speed and stealth. Still, I found my way to Earwyn's tree, as it was situated between mine and the one housing the children, just as Ossian was making his way down onto the platform. Part of me wanted to fall into my husband's arms, but the other knew that I needed to acknowledge the help that had miraculously arrived.

"Ossian," I greeted him. "You came." I tried to hide my shock, but it was there; the Aolani were the allies I had least expected based on how we had left things.

Ossian bowed his head a little, a hand over his heart. "It felt like my duty."

Again, much different from the tune he had sung back on the island. Perhaps the encounter with the liopleurodon had shown him just how at-risk his people were; if Ulmos could send a flesh-eating monster straight to the shore of their home, they could easily infiltrate their land and demand to take over. That was one reason to fight on our side, but I thought I knew another and chanced a guess. "And Tana?"

I felt Earwyn's gaze on my face; he was as curious and worried as I was.

A small smile crossed Ossian's lips, admittedly the first I had ever seen grace his stern, severe face. "She's well," he said with a nod. "And soon, I'll have a child to go home to, so why don't we end this once and for all?"

As much as I wanted to celebrate, there would hopefully be time for that later. "Yes, let's." I looked to Earwyn with a nod, which was much less than I wanted to give him, and said, "I'm going to feed our son. I'll be back soon."

CHAPTER TWENTY-SEVEN

EARWYN

I took the first shift for the group in my tree, settling in with Ossian by my side. We didn't speak much, aside from him introducing me to another Aolani, who landed on the platform next to me so stealthily that I hadn't noticed them at first.

"This is Aithne," Ossian told me, gesturing to the soldier. "The captain of our army and my strongest fighter. I'm entrusting them with leading us to victory."

Aithne was tall, probably only a couple of inches shorter than myself, and towered over Ossian. They were leanly muscled like the rest of the Aolani army, but instead of being shirtless, they wore what resembled a leather tank top with a low front that exposed the striations and separation of their pectoral muscles. They had a soft face with high cheekbones, and their dark hair was styled short in the front, with a messy fringe and waves that framed their face, and a longer tail in the back that resembled the mane of a horse. Though their expression was stoic, their gray eyes sparkled at their leader's praise. On their belt hung a huge conch shell, no doubt the instrument that had sounded the alarm earlier. While Aithne was surprisingly still, any small movement that they made seemed to be tracked by other Aolani up in the trees, who watched them intently for directions. They would certainly give the army of Ulmos a run for their money, I thought.

"Good to meet you, Aithne." I reached out to shake their hand, and they regarded me instead with a curt nod, keeping their hands folded behind their back. I withdrew the gesture as soon as I realized it wouldn't be returned and chastised myself mentally. "I'm Earwyn," I added, stuffing my hand into my pocket. I nodded down at the otter at my feet. "This is Genny. You probably saw—"

"Mycel, yes, your queen."

Genny muttered something to me about the awkwardness of the whole interaction, and I hoped that my face wasn't turning red in response; perhaps Mycel would have been a better ambassador for our people. I could tell that the soldier wasn't interested in small talk, so I decided to keep our conversation to planning only. "Would you like to rest for this shift?"

"I'll rest when this is over. Soon, with any luck."

Ossian beamed with pride.

CHAPTER TWENTY-EIGHT

MYCEL

When I found Evren again, Neeri was asleep on her father's shoulder, and it took everything in me not to break down at our reunion. Partially because I had never been away from my child for that long, nor had I expected our time apart to be so brutal. But also because soon we'd have to part again… and it might be worse. My chest ached as I undid my armor to nurse my son on the floor of the safehouse, and when I let my head fall back against the wooden wall, I tried desperately to relax my shoulders. It didn't work.

"Mycel?" Zahir whispered from across the room.

"Mmm?" I looked up to find the young man staring at me while he stroked his daughter's hair. I imagined that was the first moment of peace and comfort they had felt since they parted that morning.

"Thatcher…" Zahir began, his voice cracking as he said his friend's name. "Is he going to be okay?"

I swallowed hard. "I'm not sure. I hope so." I squeezed my eyes shut tight and remembered scouring the woods for plants to heal Firth with. A fat tear forced its way out from between my eyelashes at my realization. "With the forest floor unreachable, I can't look for anything to help him… so if we don't already have it available, he will need to hold on until they retreat…"

When I looked over again, Zahir was nodding solemnly. "They'll retreat," he said, clearly trying to convince himself.

I looked down at Evren and stroked his blond hair as he nursed. "They'll retreat," I echoed. When he was full and sleepy, I reluctantly passed him off to Zahir, who let the little boy sleep on his free shoulder without complaint. It took me more than a minute to fully let go of him, my fingertips lingering on my son's back as he snuggled into our friend's neck, and then I forced myself to replace my armor before heading back to the battle.

* * *

When our enemies descended again, they came in the water they had flooded our home with, the water that none of us could enter due to its toxicity. I wish I knew more about it and what made their selected Ulmosi resistant to its harshness as well as what it was doing to the forest. Would the earth beneath us be damaged permanently? Would the trees fall later because they'd been soaking in toxic sludge? It was proof, again and again, that Ulmos did not care for the earth that they inhabited, nor the creatures. They would use whatever means to get what they wanted, even if it left death and destruction in its path, even if it wiped out entire races in the process.

As they closed in on us, we attempted to plan.

"I can take some of them out before the water gets to me," Rhodes offered, already pulling off his shirt to prepare to jump into the water.

"No," Earwyn said firmly, and I thought I saw a twinge of concern in his fair face. "You'll be dead before you get close enough, especially if you're breathing it through your gills." For a moment I imagined the agony of breathing burning liquid; I didn't doubt that Rhodes would do it if we asked him to, but we couldn't. He wouldn't just be in pain like Owen and Thatcher; he would die. Earwyn would never let himself live down the loss of both brothers.

Meanwhile, the polar bears looked at each other hopelessly, well aware that they were at risk of being injured just like their brother and father if they jumped in.

"We can take them out from the trees," Aithne offered, arms folded across their chest as they surveyed the water below.

Then, Agnes piped up. "It won't be enough."

Aithne looked offended at the suggestion. "And why not?"

"There are too many. We're outnumbered." Agnes shook her head in frustration; she'd obviously been watching closely from her post. Not only did the Ulmosi have more resources at their disposal, they had more people overall. The sea was far vaster than a single forest in the Pacific Northwest, after all. Who knew how many other oceanic terrafolk they'd recruited for their fight.

"What's your idea?" I asked, knowing full well that we didn't have time to dance around the details.

"Let me down. I can stop them," she told the group, her voice quiet but certain.

"You won't survive the water."

"I only need a few seconds, then get ready to pull me back up." Oona squealed from her person's shoulder. "It's the only way to slow them down; otherwise we're just prolonging the inevitable. They will get to the trees and overpower us. There are just too many."

I looked from Agnes to her mother, worry certainly streaking my face. Nora was clearly fighting back tears at the idea of another one of her children being hurt, but I knew she trusted her judgment. Still, she was just a child. "I know it'll work." Nora nodded. What she didn't say, however, was that the cost may have been too great.

"If we're going to do this, we'd better do it now," Rhodes grunted. "They're getting closer."

Moments later found us watching from our platform as one of the

Aolani soldiers escorted Anges down a tree toward the water, which was practically bubbling with approaching bodies. They filled the flooded spaces, swimming, paddling, dipping, and diving, all headed for the surrounding trees.

I was close enough to hear Agnes tell the soldier, "Be ready to pull me back up, please… and quickly." Oona flew overhead.

The second Agnes's feet dipped into the water, she struggled to bite back her reaction to the pain. Soon she was chest deep and panting. She opened her mouth and let out a yell that was suited for someone much, much larger than herself and plunged her hands into the water at her sides. She was right – it took only a matter of seconds before ice splintered out from every side of her body, causing the water to freeze around her. The ice shot through the water, solidifying it as far as the eye could see, and as a result it froze every single Ulmosi intruder that was touching the water as well; most were beneath, but some had been mid-movement and half out. They were locked in place as well, looks of horror and panic etched on their previously smug faces. The ice must've built up beneath Agnes because she rose higher and higher until she reached up again to grab the soldier's arm. Once he had her secured, the young girl fainted.

Rhodes was on standby to help the Aolani soldier get Agnes back up into the tree, and he carried her promptly into the closest dwelling for medical support. I didn't know what that would look like, but had no time to wonder, because the forest soon filled with the crunch of heavy boots along the ice. It was thick and would not crack, thanks to Agnes's work, but the next wave of Ulmosi were approaching.

As they got closer, however, we could see that they were struggling to traverse the new terrain of the forest. They were slipping, their metallic shoes causing them to slide across the ice despite their attempts to march straight on through. We had the advantage here; Yannavi shoes were leather, grippy, and pliable so that they could easily climb trees and navigate stones and roots throughout the woods. Our Aolani brothers were barefoot. They'd likely be cold, but the ice wouldn't be as slick for them as it was for the enemy. Their archers would remain in the trees, while those wielding swords would accompany us on the ground.

Earwyn and I looked from each other to Aithne, and each gave the silent cue for our people, including ourselves, to drop from the trees onto the ground and brace for their approach. They would be slower, due to the ice, and we needed any additional time we could get to steady ourselves.

"Yannavi, Aolani, my Alaskan family," I addressed our group, projecting my voice as far as it would go. "Hold steady. They have taken enough from us; give them nothing more. We will not kneel."

Though I had fully expected to see Maren at some point, I hadn't expected her to be first to approach on the ice, flanked by her soldiers who looked to be struggling miserably under their heavy armor. She wore something lighter, of course, steel that had been hammered so thin I wasn't sure how it could possibly protect her, and in true Maren fashion, it was decorated with pearls and gems. Also unsurprisingly, she didn't bother with any sort of head protection so that her hair, piled high in an intricate hairdo as usual, could be witnessed by all. A bold move, I thought, considering she was a target for so many. Despite being less weighed down than her army, she still struggled to traverse the ice. Somehow she held herself upright, though I was convinced the soldiers behind her were keeping her steady.

I didn't give her a chance to speak. Instead, I held my head high and addressed her directly. "Surrender. Surrender or every Ulmosi under the ice will die, Maren." Sure, they could breathe underwater, but there wasn't a single ounce of liquid left beneath the surface; Agnes had filled their lungs with ice. They would suffocate if Maren didn't act quickly.

"You should know better; I always get what I want. There's no chance in hell that I'm leaving here without it."

Maz stayed on my shoulder, his beady eyes narrowed in her direction. *She doesn't care, Mycel. She'll let them die and feel nothing.*

When Earwyn drew his sword and pointed it at his ex-fiancée, the tyrant ruler of his old people, his abuser, his nightmare, I should've expected her reaction.

She laughed.

"Move in," she snipped, gesturing for those Ulmosi behind her to attack. They charged forward, and we clashed into each other like waves over rocks, the carnage I had been fearing all along unfolding in a matter of seconds. Yannavi and Aolani soldiers alike faced off against the Ulmosi guards, each group meeting the weapon-end of the others. Some fell quickly, the brute strength of each side too much to fight against, while others locked into duels one-on-one. All around me, our friends fell, but not before dealing blow after blow to those around them. It would have been a sight to any humans, seeing us go against each other for so long; soldiers would fall, injured in a way that would easily kill a human, then rise again once their wounds had magickally healed. It was only when the opposing side dealt a blow to a vital organ or slit someone's throat that they would be gone for good. Then they fell again, permanently, the thick ice the only thing separating them from all of the other casualties the battle had already produced. It was poetic, in a way, that they were laid to rest so close to each other.

I didn't see Zara anywhere. I would have panicked more if I had time, but as I searched the area for her, another Ulmosi soldier charged at me. I hardly had a chance to raise my sword before I was thrown backward onto the ground by the blow. Before I could scramble to my feet, Rhodes was in front of me, lifting the soldier off the ground by the throat before snapping the man's neck and discarding him. Something about the way he moved suggested he had been waiting for this moment for a very, very long time. "Th-thanks."

Rhodes offered me nothing more than a grunt as he ran off to chase down another guard who had noticed him and immediately attempted to flee. "Not so fast!" The ice crunched and splintered under his heavy steps.

The polar bears ganged up on groups of Ulmosi, tearing them limb from limb together. Their screams echoed through the depths of the forest as arms, legs, and hands were scattered upon the icy ground, leaving streaks and splatters of blood and viscera as they were tossed aside. One of them – I couldn't tell who from a distance – crunched an ankle in his vise of a mouth as he chased down another Ulmosi soldier, whose panicked yelling was stifled only when he slipped and hit his head on the ice.

Someone, somewhere, had identified the tree where Evren, Neeri, and other vulnerable Yannavi were being kept and sent a group of Ulmosi up to scale it. Thankfully, they were slow due to their lack of familiarity with climbing trees. I yelled for Aithne, for Ossian, and screamed that they had to protect that tree at all costs, and the Aolani archers quickly struck down almost all enemy soldiers within ten feet of it. One particularly adept Ulmosi soldier, however, managed to dodge several arrows, hiding behind the tree's trunk as he scaled its surface. I made a run for the tree, grateful for the soles of my shoes for allowing me some sort of traction on the thick ice, but met the blade of a sword on my way and was forced to engage with it.

"Zahir!" I screamed, noticing the Aolani man from the corner of my eye as I blocked each jab from my attacker. He didn't even have to look twice to see what I was worried about and sprinted across the ice, unbuckling the ax from his arm to toss it on the ground as he approached the tree and then chasing the Ulmosi soldier up with impressive speed; he had the advantage here. When he caught up with the soldier, he struggled to pull a weapon from his belt. With no other option in sight, Zahir grabbed on to the attacker, the man who would put our children in danger, and pulled him off of the tree, sending them both plummeting to the ground. There, he reconnected with his weapon, grimacing in pain as he grabbed the handle and then swung it directly into his victim's head.

Maren, of course, had chosen to lock on to Earwyn. I sprinted back toward him and was halted by another soldier who pointed a sword at my throat. I knocked it away with my own, only to find that I was surrounded. Earwyn had his weapon pointed at Maren, but she was staring him down mercilessly as if she were invincible.

"Isn't this a familiar arrangement?" Maren purred, clicking her tongue as she closed the gap between herself and my husband. "You being held down so I can have my way with you. This will be our last playtime, though, I'm afraid… Once I have your little mutt, I won't need you anymore."

Earwyn grunted against his captors, who held a blade to his throat. I was so close. I could help. I could free him from this hellish tormentor forever.

"I dream about watching you die," he bit out.

"Too bad that dream won't ever come true."

"I wouldn't speak so soon."

As if on cue, Zara dropped from a tree above, landing so close to Maren that she hardly had time to react. Zara didn't skip a beat, lunging toward the other woman and plunging her shortsword directly into Maren's neck, downward into her chest. The weapon squelched and crunched, and I marveled at how strong Zara must've been to drive it into her body so efficiently… either how strong or how full of rage. Had she stayed up in a tree until just the right moment, waiting? Maren kept herself upright for longer than expected, her eyes wide in shock, as she reached for the blade in her neck and felt around for it aimlessly. Her mouth gaped as she fought for air, but crimson soon stained her lips, and she fell onto her knees.

I took the opportunity to overpower my shocked captor and knock them to the ground, then pointed my own blade at the soldier, whose hands immediately went up in surrender.

"Z? Earwyn? You okay?" I didn't dare look their way again, afraid that I might be overpowered by the soldier who I finally had the upper hand with.

"Good," Zara replied, her own shock apparent in her voice.

All Earwyn managed was a clear "Yeah."

CHAPTER TWENTY-NINE

ZARA

The forest spun around me as I watched the light fade from the eyes of the woman I'd just stabbed. Part of me felt sick, queasy, and like I wasn't in control of my own body. The other part, the part I listened to, told me to pull my sword out of her neck and kick her body to the ground. So I did. It slurped loudly on its way out and caused blood to gush from Maren's neck. When she fell sideways onto the ground, propelled by my foot, she twitched as she bled onto the ice. Then she was still.

I pointed my sword at the men behind Earwyn. He was looking from the dead body on the ground to me and back again in shock. God, I really hoped he didn't want to talk about this. Honestly, I didn't have the capacity to discuss these things any more. All I knew was that now that the guard and the queen who were responsible for Firth's death, for Earwyn's abuse, for the torturous chase of my best friend and her child were dead, I could die happily if that was my fate.

"Let him go," Mycel's voice sounded from nearby as she threatened her own Ulmosi guard. "Tell them to stand down. Your old leader is dead."

When I glanced around, I found the ground littered with bodies from both sides. But the Ulmosi who were still standing were at the mercy of the Yannavi, Aolani, and Alaskans that had their weapons poised to kill. There was nothing left to do but surrender.

"Retreat," the soldier in front of Mycel choked out. "Fall back. Fall back!"

The second they showed signs of fleeing, I took inventory of the people I loved. Mycel and Earwyn were nearby, the bears I could see were breathing… Zahir, too… where was Reed? A groan caught my attention, and I raced toward the sound. If this asshole died in my arms, I was going to be very upset with him. I found Reed upright against a tree, groaning as he gripped his shoulder; he'd been stabbed.

"Is it over?" he asked, wincing.

I kneeled in front of him, unsure of what to do. "Yeah, it's over."

"Good," he said with a sigh, then let his head fall back against the tree. "I won our bet."

"What are you talking about? You're bleeding everywhere!"

"Sure, but I ain't dead. That was the whole deal. Besides, it's just a scratch, it's hardly worse than when Earwyn beat the shit out of me for gawking at you during the wedding… and isn't this kinda thing sexy? You know, fighting for what's—"

"Gawking at *me* during the wedding?" I kissed his stupid face.

CHAPTER THIRTY

MYCEL

Once our attackers had backed away, retreated in defeat, Earwyn and I returned to the treehouse that had kept our tiniest loved ones safe along with the elders and reunited with our son. I held my breath as we climbed up into the treehouse, Earwyn still a little less adept at scaling trees without a ladder or steps, and knocked in the pattern we'd agreed upon prior to the start of the fight. Betulia, the elder who had officiated our wedding, opened the door for us with Neeri peering around her past the large swaths of fabric that made up her skirt.

"What news?" she asked, her gaze hopeful and serious.

She didn't fully open the door until I said, "They're gone."

"And my daddy?" Neeri asked curiously as we entered the house.

"He's safe, sweet girl. I know he'll be here any minute."

Before we could exchange any further news, Neeri had bolted further into the house and returned happily carrying my son, who had clearly just been woken from another nap; I was grateful for just how oblivious to all of the madness around him Evren had been. "Did you hear that, Evren? The bad guys are gone, and everyone is okay!"

Earwyn tensed next to me at her last statement, knowing full well that there were many injuries and losses to account for. We were grateful that those who had been unable to fight – our children and elders – had been protected by that immeasurable sacrifice of others. Neeri and Evren never saw a single scratch. When Earwyn took our son into his arms from a giddy and relieved Neeri, the little boy reached up with a tiny hand to rest it on his father's cheek, reminding me of how quickly terrafolk babies develop. Their reunion was sweet enough that it made all of the risk, all of the pain, worth it.

SUMMER

CHAPTER THIRTY-ONE

EARWYN

It was the start of summer before Yannava returned to any semblance of its real self again; the war, the battles, they had done harm to the forest and our people that took many months to heal. The trees that remained standing eventually strengthened their roots, and others grew where smaller, weaker trees had fallen. The forest did bloom, just later than usual, and animals rebuilt their homes in it. Our people, too, rebuilt their dwellings. We did not move those ground dwellings up into the trees for fear of future flooding as an act of defiance; there would be no Ulmosi attacks again because Evren Firth was the rightful king to that throne, and he would never allow such terror to occur again. Ulmos, meanwhile, awaited my return. I prayed that my parents shook in fear every day when they thought about me coming home.

Some of that damage was irreversible, however. We had lost count-less lives.

Thatcher, Owen, and Agnes all sustained lasting injuries from the effects of the tarnished water; the flesh that it had touched had been permanently scarred and caused them regular pain. We offered them permanent homes in our city so that they wouldn't have to trek back to Alaska until they were ready. The other bears returned home to see their wives and children, but Nora stayed behind. They haven't decided when they'll leave, but our doors will forever remain open to them. Zahir decided to stay wherever Thatcher would be and professed his love to the other young man when he was bedridden and bandaged, so Neeri stayed with them, too.

Reed's shoulder healed, but the injury caused him limited mobility in one of his arms. He thought the scar was cool.

We let the Ulmosi claim their dead, and some did, faces I recognized from my time in the sea. But no one came for Maren. Her body lay in the middle of our city, avoided by all like the plague, until Mycel took it upon herself to burn her rotting body somewhere deep in the woods. She gathered some of the ashes and gave them to me with a knowing look in her eye; I'd bring those back to Ulmos with me.

We eventually pulled Hyssop's body from the thawing ground. Her neck was black and blue with the bloodied new gills that the Ulmosi had given her and had ultimately led to her suffocation and death. Mycel regarded the retrieval with a somber intensity that I couldn't quite read, but when Clove saw her wife, she screamed so loud that the birds fled every tree nearby. Mycel held her close and stroked her hair as she sobbed. We buried Hyssop like the rest of our people, forcing ourselves to forgive her even when it seemed impossible. I told myself that, if I could put Maren's memory to rest, I could do the same with Hyssop. Too much of my life had been ruled by these people. They were finally gone.

When the warmth of summer crept in, before Ossian, Aithne, and Nora left, we allowed ourselves a moment to breathe. We gathered on a summer evening in the same place where many lives had been lost not long before and filled the air with laughter and quiet conversation. Evren crawled through the grass and moss that now covered the ground, which was slowly but surely repairing itself, and Boone followed behind, chasing his feet as they wiggled through the dirt. For the first time since I had learned of his existence, I wasn't worried about my son's safety. I kept an eye on him, sure, but we were surrounded by friends and allies.

We gathered around a massive table that was covered with food made from summer in the woods: pasta with chanterelles, smoked salmon, cake made with chocolate mint, and pies of every berry imaginable, among other treats. People dressed in a variety of clothing. Some were just glad to be able to dress normally without having to prepare for war, while others dressed up. Mycel, Zara, and Agnes had been gifted beautiful gowns by our people, and Mycel looked particularly stunning in a beaded green number that made her emerald eyes even more enchanting. I watched her intently from across the table as she toasted with those around her: Clove, Elan, Zara, Agnes, and Nora were closest.

Evren took breaks from his exploring to sit on her lap to nurse or grab at her food, which he then threw down to Boone on the ground. At one point he crawled over to Rhodes, who sat next to me, and put his arms up toward the other man while grabbing at the air. He whined, and when a sudden sneeze erupted from his tiny face, the action caused flowers to bloom suddenly all around him; his magick was clumsily arriving.

"What do you want, kid?" Rhodes asked with a grunt, then looked at me when he remembered that the little boy couldn't very well explain himself. "The hell does he want?"

I was about to explain when Zara burst into laughter.

"What?"

"He wants you to pick him up, you big oaf," Zara informed him, wiping the corners of her eyes as her laughter calmed. "You know, 'uppies.'"

Rhodes's eyes widened in shock, and to my surprise, he eventually reached down and picked up my son. The little boy settled happily into his uncle's lap, where he pulled on the man's beard before making a grab at a dinner roll on his plate. "Hey!" he scolded him, snatching the piece of bread back immediately. But when Evren's lower lip jutted out in a pout, he relented. "Fine…" They spent the rest of the evening bickering with each other as much as a baby and a grown man could, but Rhodes made no attempt to set him back down. He even tried to show the boy how to conjure a small stream of water by channeling the Ulmosi side of his magick, and they both laughed when Evren accidentally squirted Boone in the face.

CHAPTER THIRTY-TWO

ZARA

The forest was just starting to heat up when the world of Yannava seemed to right itself again, and though I was enjoying what life could look like after so much chaos and loss, I still felt overwhelmed. I slipped away from dinner to spend some time alone. To process. To breathe. It would be a long time yet before things felt like any sort of "normal" for me and that was something I had come to terms with.

Still, I settled into a routine. I moved my body. I breathed the forest air. I learned how to exist in Yannava's world, finding my place and ways to contribute. I spent time with my friends, and I babysat, as much as you can babysit a magickal baby. I made tea and drew in a journal that I crafted myself with the help of some Yannavi women.

"I've been patient, but I won that bet fair and square." Reed's voice came from behind me as I milled about in the woods, desperate for a bit of air after so much close contact with everyone in the village. When he dropped down from the branch of a tree I had passed, then spun me around with a strong hand, his gaze searched my face. His brow furrowed. "Unless, of course, you're no longer interested. In which case, I'll disappointedly but respectfully fuck off."

I sighed. The weight of his hand on my shoulder sent a chill through my body, even with the sticky summer air. "It's not that."

When he tipped my chin up with a thick, rough finger, my knees threatened to buckle. "What is it, then?"

I felt stupid for what I was about to say, but it had been on my mind for longer than I cared to admit. "What if it ends?"

"It could, it might," Reed told me with a half-smile. "There's no telling when or how it will. But to truly enjoy it, you have to try to be present without letting those questions plague ya. Be here, right now, with me. Enjoy it whether it lasts a moment or a millennium. I can tell ya with confidence that this won't be a one-time thing if I have anythin' to say about it."

I sighed again. "Reed, I'm not Mycel."

Reed sucked his teeth and shrugged; he winced a little as he did so, his wound still sore even after weeks. "Well, darlin', I'm not Firth. I'm not tryin' to be."

Something about that statement was oddly reassuring. He wasn't Firth, he would never be, but he wasn't trying to fill that hole in my heart. He was just trying to be part of it, somehow, in his own unique way. I didn't have to compare him to anyone else or feel remorse, as if I were allowing him to take the place of my long-lost lover, because it wasn't like that. I smiled up at him, a rarity for me in those times, and stood on my tiptoes to press a brief kiss to his mouth. He tasted like rosehips. When I pulled away, he caught me by the wrist. "I want more," he told me, his gaze predatory and hungry. He pressed a kiss to my palm before letting me loose.

"More, huh?" I couldn't help but smirk when I challenged him. "Well, you'll have to catch me first."

The man's eyebrows shot up in surprise, but he was quick to respond. "Before you run, you should know what you're running from," Reed warned, his tone suddenly dangerous. The lighthearted flirtiness had left him in a rush, and when he yanked his shirt over his head, exposing a thick, rigid body with slabs of muscle that looked like they could crush a skull with ease, I shivered. Dark hair, speckled with gray, dusted his pecs down to the waistband of his pants, where it disappeared into his slacks. I'd seen that exact sight a few times already, when I'd fallen asleep next to him because I needed the comfort of his warmth and presence… but back then, I hadn't really let myself appreciate it. He was big and strong and not to be fucked with, but God, I couldn't wait to fuck with that. Heat spread between my thighs.

"And this." He grunted, grabbing my hand, which looked like a doll's compared to his. He pressed my palm against the front of his trousers, where his length was rock hard and straining against the fabric; he wanted to chase me. I gasped. He let go of me and stared down his nose when he uttered one last word in a growl: "Run."

Then I was off and grateful that he was likely to give me a small head start; he knew the woods better, he was stronger, faster, more agile even when injured. He'd seen me trip over exposed tree roots enough times to know that he had a distinct advantage. Even his stride was twice the length of mine, so I'd have to rely on my ability to hide to put off my capture for as long as possible. My mind alternated between "Oh fuck, I'm in trouble" and "I can't wait to see what he does when he finds me." I ran as fast as I could and tried to hold in the involuntary yelps that tried to escape when I thought about the fact that I was literally being chased through the woods by a huge man with a giant dick.

Soon my head start was over, and Reed took off after me. How did I know he'd started his hunt? Well… "I can smell you, Zara," he growled. The ground trembled with each of his big steps. Or was that just my shivering in anticipation? "Hell, I can't wait to lay you out and have my way with you."

I soon found that I was so giddy I could hardly keep myself upright and hid behind a towering tree to catch my breath. He was going to catch me. I put a hand over my mouth to try to muffle my panting just as his footsteps approached. He was only a few feet away when he whistled a little. "Come out, come out… I wonder…" he mused aloud, stepping closer and closer. I was trapped. Any way I could think about running would put me right in front of him, and he was able to cover ground so much quicker than me. "How do you like it? Soft and slow? Do you want to savor the stretch as you take each thick inch of me?" He turned the corner around the tree and smirked, placing his hands on the trunk on either side of my body as he towered over me. "Or do you want me to fuck you hard and deep until you scream?"

Reed stared into my eyes like he could see my every thought and smiled as he put a finger on my chin to tilt it up. "A little bit of both, maybe?" he asked, then pressed his lips to mine in a kiss that took my breath away. When the kiss broke, I slid down the tree onto my knees in front of him. He raised an eyebrow as his gaze followed me. "What are you doing?"

"You caught me," I surrendered.

"Sure… get your ass up off the ground. When I said I wanted more, I just meant more of you, not more from you."

"You don't like blowjobs?"

Reed looked confused.

Right, human phrases. I wasn't sure what they called it in Yannava. All I knew was that I was dripping wet, my heart was racing, and I was fully prepared to try to take his monster of a cock as far into my throat as I could. "You don't want me to suck your cock?"

Reed's laughter was booming; it took up as much space as his giant body. "Is that what humans call it? I don't want you to think of it as a job… and blowing?"

I snorted. "Yeah, I don't know."

"'Course I do, but you haven't even caught your breath… can't go filling up your mouth right away, huh?" The way Reed laughed this time wasn't his usual jovial chuckle but a seductive invitation. He hoisted me up off the ground and kissed me again, then grabbed my hand to place it on his belt. I got the message and undid it eagerly, like I had been starving for him all along, and gasped into his mouth when he fell into my palm. I wasn't sure how he'd fit inside me when I could barely get my hands around him, but I stroked him anyway, savoring the way he growled against my lips at my touch.

Reed made quick work of my clothes, and I only stopped touching him to give him access to them for brief seconds, so that he could yank them off and toss them onto the ground. When I was naked before him, he traced a finger between my thighs. "So wet for me already… you like being chased."

A chill ran through my body at his words, and I struggled to formulate a response. "By you, maybe."

"You hate to admit it, though."

I crossed my arms across my chest in mock defiance, and he grinned. It took him only a second, but he pulled me up into his arms, then further up his body until my legs were flung over his shoulders, my cunt only inches from his face. He looked up at me, then took a few steps so that I was against a tree. "Lean back and let me eat." I hated just how painfully handsome his face was framed between my thighs, and when I did as I was told, I hated the involuntary whimper that burst from my lips. I could feel him smiling against my flesh as he licked me, then sucked on my clit. Within seconds I was gripping his hair as he ground his face into my pussy, no doubt drenching his beard in my juices.

"Oh, fuck, Reed!"

"What was that?" Reed purred beneath me, gripping my thigh tightly with one hand while he snaked the other round to plunge two fingers into me while he lapped at my cunt.

I groaned in frustration, annoyed that he had brought me to the edge so quickly that I'd say his name. "You won't hear it again," I snipped, trying desperately not to moan. He was relentless, fucking me with his fingers.

"We'll see," he told me, his tone almost threatening. He sucked on my clit long and hard before looking up at me again. It was then that I realized he'd let go of my thigh and I was balancing solely on his massive shoulders alone. He was using his free hand to touch himself. God, that was hot. "I'm gonna come while eating your pussy. And you're gonna scream my name. Now or later, you choose."

I don't know how he did it, but he somehow managed to coordinate his fingers and tongue and hold me upright and deal with my attitude all at the same time. I gripped his hair roughly and ground myself into his face as he worked me, fisting his own cock at the same time. "Fuck, fuck, it's so good," I whined, and just as I tipped over the edge into my own orgasm, he grunted against my flesh, his muscles jerking as he came at the same time.

I slumped back against the tree, a shaking mess, and the giant Yannavi looked up at me, his beard glistening between my legs. "Later, then… and by 'later,' I mean right now."

"I can't," I told him breathlessly. "Besides, how can you—" Hadn't he just blown his load all over the forest floor?

"You think I survived a war and chased you through the woods to make you come once and send you on your way?" Reed scolded me as he pulled me off his shoulders and set me on trembling legs. I was shocked to see that he was as hard as ever, and though he rubbed his shoulder a little after letting me down, he didn't miss a beat. "Ride me, beautiful."

"You're gonna fuck your name out of me?" I quipped, but I didn't argue when he sat down on the ground, back against the tree we'd just used, and pulled me into his lap. He was so thick that my thighs trembled a little despite my attempt to remain cool.

Suddenly, his playful demeanor faltered, and he looked me in the eyes with an intense seriousness that seemed to come and go in our relationship. "You really don't want to like me, do you?" He stroked my cheek a little, then ran a thumb over my bottom lip. "Or you don't want to let yourself like me, even though I'm good for you?"

I tore my gaze away from his and reached between us to grip his cock, then rubbed it against my soaked lips before notching the head inside of me. Even that was a stretch. I winced a little.

"Look at me," Reed said suddenly, his voice commanding. His hand was still on my face, but he didn't use it to direct me and instead waited until I met his gaze on my own. His other hand went to my hip, where he stopped me from taking him any further. "It's okay," he told me. "You can let yourself be here with me, you can enjoy yourself, without it meaning something big and scary."

I grabbed his hand and put it on my chest, overwhelmed by the intensity of his directness. He kneaded my breast softly and smiled when he rolled a nipple between his rough fingers, but when I lowered myself further onto him, shifting side to side to accommodate his girth, he let his head fall back. A groan, deep and guttural like it was bordering on agony, escaped his parted lips. "Zara, that's…"

"So good," I told him as I took him to the hilt with a gasp. He throbbed and I clenched, and I met his gaze again only to be left breathless by the warmth in his eyes. Don't hide behind your grief, I told myself. I was allowed to be happy, to experience good things again. I put a hand on the back of Reed's neck and pulled him to me for another kiss, letting myself savor the way he tasted like berries and honey mead and comfort. I pulled up off of him, delighting in the way the thick head of his cock massaged just the right parts inside of me, and whimpered into his mouth. "It's too good, Reed…" I panted. He didn't tease me for saying his name.

CHAPTER THIRTY-THREE
MYCEL

The celebration had ended, and we'd sent our guests off on their journeys when Earwyn, Evren Firth, and I finally retired to our treehouse. I'd seen Zara take off earlier, and Reed had followed sometime after that. I knew that they were fond of each other, could feel it whenever they were near one another, and honestly, I was happy for them. Why wouldn't I be? They were both more than deserving of love and companionship, and I could not have thought of two people who were better suited for each other, especially after all they had been through. I hoped that Reed would be someone for Zara to heal with… and that Zara could bring out and embrace Reed's fun-loving and lighthearted side, which was challenging for him to access, given the serious nature of his job.

It still felt unreal that my husband and I could fall asleep next to each other, with our son nearby, and no threat of danger or war on the horizon. We left the curtains of our treehouse open, and a welcome breeze fluttered in as we lay awake in bed. Nearby, a couple of candles flickered with the shifting air. The hum of the summertime forest filled the air, and Evren shifted occasionally in his sleep, murmuring here and there, or pulling Boone closer to snuggle with. I had spent many nights following the final battle waiting for something else to happen, for hell to be unleashed upon us again, for more loss to plague our people and our family. But it never came. I knew better than to think challenges would never cross us again, but for now, life was peaceful.

"Goddess?" Earwyn asked in the dark.

"Wyn?"

"I need to go back," he told me gently. "It's been weeks, and I have no idea what the state of the city is. I don't know what's happened to my parents and…"

"You don't know if we'll have to fight for your place… or Evren's place there." In truth, he was the rightful heir to both thrones, but if Earwyn's parents were still ruling as they had been before, they were likely unprepared to concede.

He nodded, and I rolled over to face him. The moonlight shining through our window cast a beam of illumination across his handsome face. He looked different, older than when we had first met. Whether it was the stress of all we'd been through or his time without magick, I couldn't tell, but I knew that our experiences together had changed us. "Are you worried?" I asked. "About seeing them."

Earwyn smiled in the darkness, and I reached out a hand to stroke his cheek. He placed one of his hands over mine and pressed it close to his skin. "Worried? I don't know if that's the word… but this seems like the final piece in closing this chapter. Ulmos needs to be managed, planned for. It needs to recover, and they can't be trusted with that task themselves."

"I love you."

My husband laughed a little. The sound filled me with warmth and made my limbs tingle. "Yeah? Where did that come from?"

"I haven't told you enough. There have been so many times where we've almost lost each other," I recounted, still coming to terms with just how much we'd been through together. I swallowed hard. "And I just… I haven't told you enough. I never want you to forget how much I love you… how much our son and our people love you."

"I love you, goddess."

Moments later he was pulling me down the steps of our treehouse after we'd confirmed that Evren Firth was sleeping deeply enough for us to slip out, our familiars remaining behind as a baby monitor. "Where are we going?" I whispered harshly in the night air, trying not to giggle when we hit the forest floor and he kept pulling me. "What's the rush?"

"If I'm leaving in the morning," he said, breathless with his own stifled laughter, "I need tonight with my wife."

Excitement coursed through my body at his words, but when was I not brimming with desire for my husband? We'd just slipped outside the edge of the city when the sound of running water hit me, and I realized that we were headed toward a stream. We'd spent so long being fearful of the water, worried about what lurked beneath, that Earwyn had been kept from his element. In fact, I couldn't recall a time in our relationship where he'd been allowed unbridled rein over his magick. "I can't imagine how you've missed the water."

Earwyn's gaze in the moonlight was mischievous. "Sure, I have, but there's one thing in particular I've been dying to do since we met." He didn't wait for my response before he pulled me into a kiss so sweet and gentle that I could not have imagined what was coming next. There was something sublime and unique about being able to make love to your husband without worrying about his secrets, wondering why you're losing your magick, trying to get in a quick fuck before you're executed, or waiting for war… something comfortable and safe and warm and… he took his time kissing me all over, making me comfortable until he dropped to his knees in front of me. He worked my pants off, then my underwear with his teeth, all while gazing at me as if I were the most beautiful creature on the planet. My clothes, aside from my top, landed in a pile on the riverbank, and he nuzzled my mound, then licked at me languidly while I stood in front of him.

I didn't know what to expect when my husband instructed me to bend over in front of him, and I felt fully on display when I complied, the warm night air snaking between my bare inner thighs, which were already wet just from Earwyn's commentary. He grunted as he roughly palmed the cheeks of my ass, and I gasped when he spread them a little, much to my surprise. "Can I touch you here? Can I taste you here?" His voice was gruff, husky in the way that I'd learned meant he was hard as stone and trying to contain himself. There was something painfully sexy about the way he couldn't control himself without making it clear that it was effortful for him.

"Anywhere," I panted, leaning back into his touch. "Everywhere."

As ready as I was, I gasped again when he leaned down and buried his face in my rear, licking me from bottom to top, then lapping at the tight ring of muscle I'd never considered giving him access to. He ate me there until I was soaking wet and pressing myself against his handsome face, shocked at the sensation and nearly delirious from my uninhibited moaning. "Ah, god, Earwyn…"

"Hang on, baby," Earwyn instructed, pulling away for a moment.

"I don't have anything to hang on to," I whined, frustrated at the loss of contact.

"Shhh…" I couldn't see what he was doing behind me, but the trickle of the stream seemed magnified. I looked back to see my husband crooking a finger at the river, causing a jet of water to travel in the air from the river to between us, where it snaked between my thighs and ran itself against my clit. Again, I gasped. I dug my nails into the ground beneath me as the trickling water pulsed against my most sensitive part, almost immediately bringing me to the edge. "How's that?"

Hadn't I heard of humans using a shower head to pleasure themselves? Fuck, this was a million times better. I cried out.

"Good, huh? I'm glad… can you come like that for me?"

"Uh… uh-huh," was all I could manage.

"Perfect," Earwyn murmured, praising me as he ran his hands along the curve of my ass again. Before he dipped his face between my cheeks once more, he commanded, "Then come."

I did. For him. "Oh, god, Earwyn, please!" My climax tore through my body like a raging storm, and I leaned back against his mouth as he fucked me deep with his tongue, the stream of water never relenting against the bundle of nerves between my thighs. I quivered and cried out, digging my fingers so deep into the earth I almost thought I'd become one with it.

In typical Earwyn fashion, he leaned over me and held me close to his body as I calmed, the stream between my thighs relenting momentarily, but only enough for him to make the next move. "Again?" he asked, his voice playful and curious. I could barely squeak out a nod of agreement when he snuck his fingers into either side of my top and tore it open, freeing my breasts. I felt exposed, completely, there in the woods with my tits and ass out, the rest of me barely covered by what was now a torn scrap of fabric. He snapped his fingers, and the assault on my clit continued, but now accompanied by matching sensations that caressed and squeezed and massaged my nipples.

"Oh… God, Earwyn, what are you doing?"

"Making sure you don't forget me while I'm on my trip, goddess," he said confidently, and I heard the sound of his trousers unzipping behind me. When they were undone, his length fell against my ass, hot and hard and throbbing for me.

"I could never… oh!" I practically squealed as the streams synched up, massaging my clit and nipples in perfect unison.

Earwyn laughed to himself and placed a hand on my hip, guiding me back onto him. "Are you ready for me?"

"I don't think I could be more ready," I told him, my voice pleading. I was already so close to coming again, I feared that just another touch could send me over the edge. I tried to stave it off.

"Goddess, I want you to come so hard you're not ready to go again until I get back." He pushed into me, and I adjusted to give him access until he was fully seated inside of me. I clenched around him involuntarily and whimpered at the sensation of being so full of him, having taken him to the root already. "So warm and tight," he marveled aloud.

It felt dangerous for me to move, but I did, sliding off of him a bit and then back on until he got the message that I needed more. More. More. More of Earwyn, more of my husband, my king, always. "I've got you," he told me, thrusting into me until he found a pace that made my toes curl.

"You've – been – thinking – about this – since we – met?" I panted as he rammed into me, struggling to keep my eyes from rolling back into my head as Earwyn and his magick overwhelmed my senses. Nothing existed outside of the two of us.

"Mmm," Earwyn grunted, his fingers flexing against my hips. "It's better than I could've imagined. Ah, fuck, goddess. I'm close."

"Please," I whimpered, desperate for him to feel even an ounce of the pleasure I was being bombarded with.

He quickened his pace, his fingers digging into my hip in a way that bordered on painful, and then pulled out of me just to press his cock between my cheeks as he unleashed thick, hot ropes of come along my tender flesh. I whined and panted, pressing back into him again, desperate for the heat of him filling me. "Don't worry, goddess," he assured me as he plunged back into me again, still hard and throbbing. He sheathed himself within me again, so deep that I could feel him in my belly, and told me, "I know you like to come on my cock." Before I could reply – not that I would have formulated a response that was witty or sexy – he pushed a finger into my ass, fucking his come into me with it just as his magick sent me hurtling over the edge of my orgasm and into oblivion. Every fiber in my body tightened, squeezing his dick and his fingers and the breath from my lungs as I came with a thready cry that echoed through the woods.

When we were done, Earwyn pulled my boneless and ragged body into the stream with him, where he washed me lovingly before we rolled out onto the bank, naked. We lay in the warm grass by the trick-ling stream, marveling at the stars above us, and I hoped that Ulmos would be kind to him.

CHAPTER THIRTY-FOUR

EARWYN

"You can kick them into the bubble, and I'll be there ready and waiting to eat them," Rhodes offered as we left Yannava the next morning. We had to go alone. As much as it would have made sense to introduce my wife and son to the Ulmosi properly, I just didn't know what to expect from them. Mycel's gills had long since healed, and Evren Firth's had not shown themselves yet. Ulmosi babies got them early, but there wasn't any known history of a Yannavi and Ulmosi baby, and as such, nothing to reference for his development. He was comfortable around water, sure, but not enough for me to risk having Rhodes pull him through the ocean and hope he showed up alive on the other side.

"Sounds great, totally in line with us trying to reclaim our city and show the people we're trustworthy and different than previous rulers," I told him, throwing a small bag of supplies over my shoulder. I'd packed lightly, convincing myself that that would ensure my swift return earthside.

"Yeah, whatever. They probably taste like shit anyway." We walked in silence for a good while before he commented again. "What do you mean 'we'?"

When I didn't reply, he grabbed my shoulder to stop me. It was still hard for me to look Rhodes in the eyes, even after Firth had been gone for so long. "It's up to you, Rhodes," I told him seriously. "But Ulmos needs someone to watch over it... and I can't trust anyone there. You know that."

He opened his mouth to argue, and I cut him off promptly. "Don't decide yet," I told him. "But I know you miss the ocean. I have a feeling you're secretly dying inside on this diet of mushrooms and berries."

Conversation squashed, we covered ground quickly and found our way to a deserted beach. It was hard to vanish into the water with a shark man without people noticing, so we had to do our research when selecting a place to leave from. Rhodes's varispirit form made the trip to the shimmering city in the sea quick, which was both a blessing and a curse, but ultimately gave me very little chance to turn back. I was surprised to find that the city didn't shimmer quite as much as it used to when we approached... and that the guards at the entrance let us in immediately and without questioning. We were escorted to the hall where Mycel had stood an informal trial in front of my parents and Maren, where Rhodes had killed Anala, and where I'd learned – under the worst circumstances – that I was going to be a father, only to find it empty. Not a soul was in sight, though the bubble in the middle of the room remained, albeit stained by algae from lack of cleaning. The throne room was in disarray, as if it hadn't been inhabited in a long time, but the guard who escorted us seemed surprised that my parents were nowhere to be found.

Rhodes cast me a sideways glance as we surveyed the empty hall. When the guard offered to find my parents, something inside of me told me that it wasn't a good idea. It wasn't up to this guard to reunite me with them.

"Their room," I said quietly, looking from Rhodes to the hall that led to the royal chambers, one of which I'd grown up in and another in which I'd been tortured repeatedly. At the end of the hall was their bedroom.

He nodded. We dismissed the guard. I pounded on the door to my parents' bedroom, and when they didn't answer, I had a good guess of what was on the other side. Rhodes kicked it open, and there they lay, together, in bed. One of each of their hands was intertwined with the other's, while their free hands held tightly to some strands of what they'd last consumed: a sea plant called Opanor. Its purplish metallic tinge still stained their lips. They stared lifelessly at the intricately carved ceiling of their chambers. They had heard that I was coming, and they had decided that death was better than having to face their son... and even in death, they clung to each other. My guess was that their bodies were still warm and that they had executed this escape plan just as we were let into the city.

For once, Rhodes looked surprised.

I swallowed hard, but I didn't enter the room. I thought about it... thought about the brief and rare moments I'd had with my parents that weren't neglectful or torturous, but they didn't amount to anything compared to the reality of my relationship with them.

As if he read my mind, Rhodes finally piped up. "Good riddance," he said toward the room, his voice much quieter than I'd ever heard it. "Good riddance," he said again when he turned to me and put his hands on my shoulders, turning me away from the sight of my dead parents. "They couldn't face you because they knew, Earwyn... they knew there was no redemption for what they'd done to you."

I couldn't find the words to respond to him, and instead, we stood in silence until he – yes, Rhodes, of all people – pulled me into a hug so tight that my breath left me all at once.

* * *

Repairing Ulmos, or planning to, was infinitely harder than repairing Yannava had been. Once my parents' bodies were removed, Rhodes and I sat down in the great hall to discuss all of the damage that needed to be undone, and somewhere in that planning, in those negotiations and brainstorming, he agreed to stay. He agreed to be the steward of Ulmos for the foreseeable future, and I entrusted him to bring justice to a society that had been so far from it for so long. Ulmos had a plethora of resources that had all been misused and hoarded solely for use by the royals, while the common people slaved away and starved in the surrounding city. We began to make things right by denying my parents a traditional Ulmosi royal burial and instead distributing the wealth that it would have cost amongst the people of Ulmos. It was a tiny gesture in the grand scheme of things, but it was a start. We also made plans to revive the Salt and Earth Alliance and use it for its intended purpose: to focus on a union between Ulmos and the humans and to propel ocean conservation efforts earthside. Finally, we planned to connect the Ulmosi government with Aolan, as they bordered each other and could work together.

I left with the promise that I would bring Evren and Mycel to Ulmos as soon as possible, and I teased Rhodes that he would get his fill of "uppies" as soon as my son could be trusted to swim the distance between his two homes. Before I left, Rhodes hugged me again. I may have been the only person on the planet to have been embraced by Rhodes of Ulmos not once, but twice.

CHAPTER THIRTY-FIVE

ZARA

"You're worried that this won't last," Reed teased me, gesturing between the two of us, "but you want me to meet your mama. I don't know about humans, but that's kind of a big deal around here, babe. I think you like me." He chuckled to himself as he folded up a couple of his shirts – I'd learned he didn't really have many, so the one he gifted me had been special indeed – and put them on the bed for packing.

"Yeah, yeah, don't flatter yourself." I rolled my eyes at the huge hunk of a man, but somewhere deep inside me, my heart fluttered at the idea of him meeting my mother. I'd waited until everything had blown over with Ulmos before writing to her, but because Yannava didn't exactly have an address, there wasn't a way for her to write back. I simply told her that I was safe and had gone on some adventures that I couldn't wait to tell her about when I saw her next, which would be very, very soon. Because Ulmos still had ties to the human world, though Earwyn and Mycel were determined to change the terms of those relationships, they had access to human currency, which they graciously gifted me so that I could visit my mother. I took it only if they agreed to buy two tickets so that I could take Reed with me; they didn't argue in the slightest. In fact, Mycel had been more than happy to oblige, and Earwyn just seemed happy to get Reed out of his sight. I hadn't decided what would happen when we returned. Would I go back to being a normal human, with a regular job and apartment again? I didn't want to leave Reed or the rest of my found family. My human life hadn't been bad. I had been blessed with so many experiences, friendships, even some fun jobs, but I had never felt as "right" or "at home" as I did with these people… and they wanted me around, they'd offered me a home, unconditionally, for however long I wanted. What more could I ask for? Maybe cell phone service in the middle of the Olympic rainforest, but other than that, not much came to mind.

"Too late," Reed said with a laugh. He pulled me close and kissed me, gentle at first, then a little deeper. He tasted like summer in the forest. I didn't know if I loved him, but he felt good. He was good to me. "I'm flattered and honored and hope I can charm your mother."

"Have you ever been on a plane?" I asked as he peppered my cheeks and neck with tiny kisses that pulled me away from my task of packing a suitcase.

"Definitely not." He snorted. "Can you imagine my big ass in an airplane seat?"

"Good, then I'm sure you'll be scared out of your mind, and I can come to your rescue for once."

* * *

UNSURPRISINGLY, MY MOTHER LOVED REED. HELL, WHO DIDN'T? IT seemed I was the only person who hadn't let myself love him from the start… except for Earwyn, maybe. I had toyed with the idea of telling my mother about terrafolk ever since I sent her the letter saying I was coming, but when Reed absentmindedly caused my mother's plants – cassava, peanut, and plantains – to grow at five times their normal rate, I figured I should let her in on the secret.

CHAPTER THIRTY-SIX

MYCEL

When Earwyn returned to Yannava, Rhodes appointed as the steward of Ulmos, we settled in once more to daily life. I was helping to unpack my husband's bag from his trip when I came upon a small, shimmering seashell. I stared at it for a few seconds, admiring the way the light streaming in through our window reflected off of the textured, pearlescent surface. Genny looked up from her spot on the floor and tilted her head at the item.

"What's this, Wyn?" I asked, holding up the tiny souvenir to the light. It was beautiful.

"Oh," Earwyn murmured with a smile. He reached out to take the shell from me and rubbed it between his fingers, then called over to the crow on the far side of our room. "Got this for you, Maz."

My familiar chittered as he flew over to us and took the little treasure in his beak. Earwyn ruffled the blue-black feathers on his head in loving admiration; though they didn't interact much directly, it was clear they had missed each other while Earwyn was gone. *For my collection.* Maz took it back over to the window above Evren Firth's crib, where he placed the small seashell on the sill next to a viridescent bead from my gown and a small, smooth pebble that my son had given him.

ABOUT THE AUTHOR

Francesca Crispo is a fantasy romance author living near Seattle, WA. She received her B.A. in English Literature from Arizona State University in 2016 and her M.Ed. from Arizona State University in 2018. When she isn't writing or running a business full-time, she enjoys spending time with her family and dogs!

facebook.com/francesca.crispo.author
instagram.com/francesca.crispo.author
tiktok.com/@francesca.crispo.author

Rabbit Heart: Book 1 of the Terrafolk Trilogy

Seaborne: Book 2 of the Terrafolk Trilogy

Beholden